WILD TEMPTATION

Wilder Irish, book five

MARI CARR

PRAISE FOR WILD TEMPTATION

"If you love this series, you'll fall in love with Lochlan and May. If you are new to the series, I hope you **pull up a stool at Pat's Pub** and take some time to connect with the Collins family." ★★★★★ *Jennifer, Goodreads*

"It has hot **steamy sex, smartly timed snarky comments,** to the general **cherished love** aspect that is normal requirement of Mari Carr." ★★★★★ *Meghann, Goodreads*

"I love to read stories that I just cannot put the book down, I **devoured this one in one sitting!**" ★★★★★ *Evita, Goodreads*

"...one of those books that is going to stick with the reader. There is just enough naughty to balance out the sweet, just enough drama to keep the happy from being overpowering." ★★★★★ *Jennifer, Goodreads*

"**Hot, hot, hot!!!!!!**" ★★★★★ *Mia, Goodreads*

"Mari Carr consistently writes terrific stories, combining **organic emotional connection** and **palpable sexual chemistry**." ★★★★★ *Laura, Goodreads*

*This story is dedicated to Sheldon, Penny, Luna, Bernie and Tux.
My constant summertime companions.*

WILD TEMPTATION

She's tied up at work...by her boss.

The last thing Lochlan wanted in a new assistant was some inexperienced, gorgeous, submissive blonde. However, a promise to a friend ensures that's exactly what he's stuck with.

May knows she's out of her league, not only in her new job, but with her boss. He makes her want things she's never considered—kinky, sensual, wicked things.

When trouble at home shows Lochlan more about May's life than she wants him to see, there's no stopping the sexy protector suddenly determined to claim not only her body, but her heart as well.

PROLOGUE

Patrick Collins rocked his infant grandson, humming softly as the tiny baby slept. Of course, he was using the word "tiny" loosely.

Patrick Lochlan Wallace had been nearly twelve pounds when he was born and, even now, at the ripe old age of three months, the chunky monkey gave no impression of slowing down when it came to growing big and strong.

Lochlan was his second namesake grandson, something that Patrick still shook his head over, though it secretly delighted him. Keira had given her brother, Tris, holy hell when he'd named one of his twin boys Padraig last year, insisting she'd always said her son would be named after him.

Patrick had intervened, telling them he was very touched by their tributes, then gently suggesting Keira use Patrick as a middle name instead. His oldest daughter had enough of her mother's stubbornness in her to use it as a first name anyway, even though the strapping baby in his arms had been called Lochlan since day one.

He ran the backs of his fingers over his grandson's rosy cheek. "You are a bonny lad, son," he murmured.

Keira claimed Lochlan was the perfect baby, sleeping through the night and rarely crying. A welcome change, she said, compared to his older sister, Caitlyn, who, at three years of age, had declared herself too old for naps and proved that it wasn't merely the twos that were terrible. Keira was currently with her daughter at a playmate's birthday party at the park, and her husband, Will, was attempting to fix some faulty plumbing at their home.

Which meant Patrick had his wee grandson to himself for a few hours.

After showing him off in the pub for a half hour or so, the two of them had come up to his apartment above to relax in Sunday's beloved rocking chair. Patrick could close his eyes and recall her sitting here with every single one of their children, rocking them as she sang them the lullaby she'd selected just for them.

Patrick had never asked Sunday how she'd decided on the songs, assuming at the time, she had just selected favorites from the radio. He regretted not asking that question now as he rocked his grandson. Sunday had loved music, all kinds, so her lullabies were pulled from every style, country, pop, folk, even movie soundtracks. What song would she have sung to wee Lochlan?

Patrick was more of a traditionalist. His singing range was limited to just a few confident notes, and his lullaby of choice had always been "Too-Ra-Loo-Ra-Loo-Ral." It was simple and reminded him of Ireland.

Patrick had already sung it to Lochlan twice, the sweet babe smiling at him as he did so. "You're a generous audience," he murmured, wiping a bit of drool away from Lochlan's mouth.

Lochlan reached out and grabbed his finger.

"*Och*, that's a strong grip. You're going to be a powerhouse someday, aren't you, my beautiful boy. Maybe you'll grow up and play professional football or hockey. Wouldn't that be something?"

Lochlan tried to direct Patrick's finger toward his mouth. He suspected the baby was teething, even though Keira insisted it was too early, claiming Caitlyn hadn't gotten her teeth until nearly eight months old.

Having just gone through all the baby days with Caitlyn, Keira was more confident as a mother this time around, thinking everything with Lochlan would be similar to Caitlyn. Patrick didn't have the heart to tell her every baby was different.

"You, my hungry boy, are getting those teeth out quick. You'll be eating steak by the week's end." He laughed at his own joke, a sound Lochlan repeated.

"Such a jolly lad. You hold on to that humor, Lochlan. It will serve you well. As will that name of yours. It's one the Vikings gave their own sons. They were powerful men as well."

He continued to rock, allowing Lochlan to suck on the tip of his index finger. When the baby bore down with his gums, Patrick chuckled, his suspicions confirmed as he felt the very beginnings of a tooth.

"Clever boy," he whispered. "You know, loch is actually the Scottish word for lake, and Lochlan means land of the lakes. I didn't mention that to your mum because she knows how I feel about the bloody Scots." Patrick winced. He'd been trying to clean up his language now that the pub and this apartment was filling up with the next generation of children. "Don't tell your mum I said bloody, eh?"

Lochlan wrapped a second hand around his finger, his grip

tighter, firmer, determined to keep Patrick's finger in his mouth.

"I suspect it's the second meaning of your name that will stick, because it also means warrior. And that's the part I want you to remember, that's the name I pray you'll grow into. Because this world needs warriors, sweet Lochlan. I don't mean the overthrowing kind, the kind who push weaker people out of their way. You can be a warrior for right, a champion, the type of person who protects those who need your help, who steps forward and does the right thing, even when it's difficult."

Patrick knew it was silly to sit here having this conversation with a baby who couldn't understand him, but it didn't matter. These were the things he wanted to say to his grandson, and he wasn't getting any younger. Sunday's untimely death by cancer when she was in her fifties had taught him a valuable lesson. Say what you have to say today because there might not be a tomorrow.

Besides, Patrick couldn't dismiss the way Lochlan was looking at him, his dark-eyed gaze locked on his face. Patrick could almost swear the baby *was* listening, that he did understand.

"You're a smart boy, Lochlan, so I'll tell you the rest of my secrets, everything I've learned in six-plus decades. Hard work never killed a man, but you have to balance that with play. I suspect your sister and those wild twin cousins, Colm and Paddy, will help you there."

Patrick continued to whisper lesson after lesson to the baby. "Your last name may be Wallace, but there's Collins' blood running through those veins too. Don't hold that part of you back. Follow your heart, embrace your passions, fall in love so hard it leaves bruises. I'm still sporting a few I got when I gave my heart to your grandma, Sunday." Patrick smiled as he said her name, and Lochlan followed suit, with a full-gums, chubby-cheeked grin.

"One last thing," he murmured softly. "Always remember that family comes first. It's the most important thing, because ultimately, it's the thing you're working so hard for. I spent long hours in that pub downstairs because I wanted my family to be provided for, to have a roof over their heads and food in their bellies. I was blessed because I loved the job, but I never forgot that, while it was my passion, it wasn't my heart. Sunday and your mom and your aunts and uncles were. My wish for you is that you find a girl like my Sunday, and have a slew of crazy, wonderful kids."

Lochlan's eyes started to close, the soft rocking and quiet whispers lulling him to sleep.

"You'll be their warrior, Lochlan. And they'll be your heart."

❧   I   ❦

"I can't believe you're deserting me," Lochlan grumbled, his chest tight, his stomach aching.

Sally merely rolled her eyes—as she'd done all morning—and grinned. "I'm not deserting you. I'm retiring."

"Same difference," he muttered.

"Maybe to a young buck like you, but for an old woman who's worked her ass off the past forty years, I'd say this retirement-slash-desertion is long overdue."

Lochlan chuckled, though it came out sounding miserable.

Sally Walters, his personal assistant for the past eight years, was the picture of prim and proper. It was rare to hear her raise her voice or use a cross tone, and even rarer to hear her curse.

"You said ass," he teased, seeking a way to lighten his mood.

She lightly slapped him on the arm. "You're a scamp. And I'll miss you, Lochlan Wallace. But I promise, I'm leaving you in good hands."

"Ah yes. The replacement."

Lochlan had started his own company, AdLoch, right out of college with loans from his father and Pop Pop. Looking back now, he figured it was love, more than common sense, that had convinced the two most important men in his life to risk a fairly substantial amount of money on the dreams and schemes of a twenty-one-year-old boy. However, that love was a two-way street, and it ensured Lochlan worked night and day for years to not only pay them back—with interest—but to prove to them their faith hadn't been misplaced.

When he was twenty-six, AdLoch had been featured in *Forbes* as one of the top five tech startups in the country. Business had soared since then, and he made his first million just a few days after his twenty-seventh birthday.

Now, at thirty-one, he'd crossed that million mark a few dozen times more, and his company had expanded beyond the borders of the United States. He'd spent the last month in London, opening his first international office.

Unfortunately, the timing on that new venture hadn't been great. Sally had told him three months earlier she was retiring this month—today, actually.

But she'd made that threat every year for the last few, and he'd always convinced her to stay—typically with a big-ass raise. He had honestly thought he'd find a way to talk her out of leaving this time, just as he had in the past.

Sally was more valuable to him than his right arm, something he told her on a daily basis. When he had announced their London trip, secretly thinking it would convince her to postpone her retirement, she'd dug in her heels, telling him in no uncertain terms she was getting too old to keep up with him. She'd held firm on the end date and he'd ventured to London alone, while Sally had remained behind to hire and train her replacement.

She'd sent him several resumes early on, but Lochlan had a

stubborn streak a mile wide. So wide, he continued to insist that she would change her mind. Sally persevered, however, and told him if he wouldn't choose her replacement, she would.

And—dammit—she had.

May Flowers. She'd actually hired him a PA named *May Flowers*.

That was as much as Lochlan knew about the woman. Given her old-fashioned name, he assumed Sally understood his preference for an older assistant, someone like her, who was efficient, no-nonsense, a straight-shooter with no family ties to prevent her from being able to keep up with him.

He'd hired Sally, his first employee, one year after launching AdLoch. She had been aged-out at her previous job a couple months before responding to his ad for an administrative assistant. She'd told him point-blank in the interview that she was the best candidate he was going to talk to for the job because of her experience, her intelligence, and her work ethic. He had interviewed four other candidates, and Sally had been right. She'd had it all over her competitors, so he'd hired her. And hadn't regretted the decision for one second.

He trusted Sally enough to know she would have searched for those same standards in her replacement, but that still didn't mean he wanted someone else. He didn't have the time or the patience to start over.

He glanced at his watch, grumpy about Sally's departure. His London trip had been extended a week longer than he'd expected, which had him arriving back at the office today, on Sally's last day.

"She's late."

Sally snickered. "I told her to come in at ten. Wanted to have you to myself for an hour to catch you up to speed on what's been happening here during your absence."

They'd already used up forty-five minutes as Sally went through everything that had happened on this side of the ocean during his time away. He now employed over fifty people, and while the buck still stopped with him, there were a lot of tasks he'd entrusted to Sally.

Those tasks would now fall to May...if she could handle them.

Once again, Lochlan felt a sinking feeling in the pit of his stomach. He honestly wasn't sure he could do this without Sally, and he hated the idea of starting over with someone new.

"This is going to be a disaster." He hadn't meant to say that aloud, but he still couldn't wrap his head around the fact Sally was really leaving.

"No, it's not. May is wonderful. She's a smart woman with enough backbone to stand up to you when needed. She won't let you run roughshod over her. That's what you need. Someone to tell you when you're being an idiot, the same way I have the past eight years."

He gave her a mischievous grin. "I'm never an idiot."

That comment produced her biggest eye roll of the morning. "Of course you are. May's been working as a personal assistant for a junior partner in a tech firm the past couple of years. She understands this business and she's a quick learner. I've been extremely impressed with her the last two weeks. She's bright—a thinker with a genuine thirst to learn. Plus, she's a darn hard worker, willing to put in overtime when needed. Last night, the two of us were here until nearly seven so that we could finish covering everything she needed to know. You'll be very pleased."

The door in the outer office opened before Lochlan could reply.

"That'll be her." Sally studied his face. "Put the scowl away and smile, Lochlan."

It took some effort, but Lochlan managed a weak grin.

The look faded the second May Flowers appeared in the doorway to his office.

"What have you done?" he whispered, his words only loud enough for Sally to hear.

Sally had been smiling at May, but her attention turned to him, her forehead creased in concern. "What?"

If May Flowers was twenty-five years old, Lochlan would eat his desk. She was a petite, willowy blonde who looked as sunny as her name sounded. She wasn't old at all. She was young and beautiful and... He searched for the word that described her best. When he figured it out, it pissed him off even more.

She looked vulnerable.

He was an asshole on a good day, barking orders like a drill sergeant. There was no way this woman could handle that...handle *him*.

He looked at Sally in disbelief. "This is a joke."

This time he didn't whisper, his words carrying to May, who'd only taken a few steps into the room before she stopped, her confused gaze traveling from Sally to Lochlan then back to Sally.

Sally's eyes narrowed at his rudeness.

Lochlan tried to get a grip. Jesus. He needed a do-over on the whole morning. He'd woken up pissed about Sally's last day, and his attitude had only gotten worse with each passing minute.

Regardless, there was no way on earth Sally thought May was a suitable replacement. The woman was...

"How old are you?" The curt question flew from his lips before he could think better of it.

"I sent you her file," Sally replied through clenched teeth.

At the same time May answered, "I'm twenty-three. I'll be twenty-four in a month."

Lochlan looked at Sally in genuine disbelief.

"Since when does a person's age matter to you, Lochlan? As you know, I was in my late fifties when you hired me." Sally's tone sounded sweet to a novice, but he knew her too well. Knew she was annoyed by the question.

No, annoyed was too mild.

She was pissed now too. He was contagious.

Sally had come to her interview and defended herself against ageism. She wouldn't abide him using May's age against her, even if May was on the other end of the spectrum.

"I sent you a detailed file about May's experience as well as her personal information, remember?" Sally was also clearly ticked off to discover he hadn't bothered to look at anything she'd sent him.

"I thought you'd change your mind." He sounded like a recalcitrant child.

"I told you I wouldn't."

"Should I..." May looked over her shoulder toward the outer office. No doubt they were making her feel like an interloper in the midst of their disagreement. "Maybe I should—"

"No," Sally and Lochlan said in unison.

He swallowed heavily and forced himself to do the right thing. "I apologize." Lochlan made up the rest of the distance between them with two long strides, coming to a stop in front of May and extending his hand. "I obviously haven't been an active part of the hiring process. As I'm sure you know, I've been in London, and clearly not paying as much attention as I should have."

May's smile seemed genuine, but when her bright blue eyes narrowed for a split second, the vulnerability he thought he'd seen melted away, and a fighter emerged. "I can assure you, Mr. Wallace, that while I'm young, I'm up to the challenge of this job."

"I was expecting...I thought..."

"You thought I was going to hire someone my age," Sally murmured. "However, given your reluctance to let me leave, I thought it best to find you an assistant who would stick around for the long haul."

He glanced over his shoulder at his former assistant, sending her an apologetic shrug of his shoulders before looking at May once more.

"So, you're May Flowers," he said, a slight grin tilting his lips.

He was relieved when his olive branch was accepted so easily. May's face blossomed into a full smile that drew his attention to her plump, rosy lips and perfectly white teeth. That smile was potent. Powerful.

"My mother made a vow at her dying grandmother's bedside, swearing that if she ever had a daughter, she'd name her after her. That promise remained even after Mom married my dad, Harvey Flowers. Great-Grandma May sounded like quite a character and she was very beloved, so I just focus on that. I suppose it could have been worse."

"True. She could have named you April Showers," Lochlan teased.

May erupted into a loud, joyful laugh that sent a jolt through his system. One that felt unprofessional and too personal.

He shut it down. Hard.

"That would have been much worse," she agreed.

"I was also named after a grandparent, my Pop Pop, Patrick. He's a character too."

May was beautiful. He wished he wasn't noticing that about her. Lochlan didn't allow workplace romances between his employees, and he held himself to the same standard. This was a place of business. Personal lives were checked at the door.

But there was something about her eyes that had him studying her face too closely.

He searched for a distraction. "I'm also no stranger to unfortunate names. My father is William Wallace."

May's eyes widened with surprised delight. "Seriously?"

Lochlan nodded. "Apparently, my paternal grandparents weren't well versed in Scottish history."

May covered her mouth with her hand, giggling. The gesture drew his attention to her bare ring finger.

Sally had hired a beautiful, unmarried twenty-three-year-old woman to be his personal assistant, knowing perfectly well that Lochlan and May would be in each other's constant company—working long days that sometimes turned into long nights, as well as the occasional trips to conferences.

Lochlan wasn't the type of boss who fell for his secretary. He wasn't *that* guy. In this day and age, he was very careful to make sure his female employees felt safe from sexual harassment in the workplace. He prided himself on that.

But even more, he needed an assistant who would be married to the job, the same way he was. Surely with May's youth came a social life, the desire to go out on dates or girls' nights out. Sally had been as boring as he was, something that came in handy for the workaholic in him.

"Well," Sally said. "Looks like the two of you are going to be just fine. I suppose that's it for me."

Lochlan looked at Sally with horror. She *really* intended to leave him.

Suddenly, he didn't give a shit *what* she'd said. May couldn't have enough experience to handle all the things he needed from her. Hell, she'd only hit the legal drinking age a couple of years ago. This was a bad hire, and now Sally was going to make him clean up the mess.

"Sally..." He struggled to come up with something to say that might persuade her to stay. Perhaps indefinitely. Or just until he retired himself.

Barring that, he needed Sally to let May down gently, admit she made a mistake in hiring her. They could find another position for her in the company, one that required less experience.

He had to make her see reason. "Listen, I was thinking—"

Sally ignored him. "You have my number, yes, May?"

May nodded. "I promise to use it only as a last resort. Mexico needs your full attention."

"Mexico?" Lochlan asked.

"I'm taking a cruise. Set sail in three days for a couple of weeks. I'm not getting the international phone plan, by the way."

"So what good is it for May to have your number?" he asked, his temper tweaked again. She was leaving the country?

Sally laughed. "I'm only going to be gone two weeks, not forever. I'm sure you and May can hold down the fort without me. Actually, I planned this trip to help you. I don't want you ringing my phone off the hook out of habit, Lochlan. This way, you two will have to figure things out on your own. It's the best way to start. Trust me."

Lochlan should have rescheduled his London trip. He hated that he'd left Sally to hire her own replacement. He glanced at May. If he'd been here, he was fairly certain she would not have been the candidate of choice. Experience ranked at the top of his list. Sally should have known that.

A phone in the outer office rang. "I'll get it. It'll give you two a moment to say goodbye," May said, stepping out of his office.

"Come here, Lochlan." Sally's arms stretched out and he stepped into them, giving her a hug, the realization that this was it finally sinking in.

"I'm going to miss you around here, Sally. You always kept me on the straight and narrow. Without you, I'm likely to fall into bad habits."

She laughed, the sound deep and rough, betraying evidence of her pack-a-day smoking habit. "You've never behaved, and you know it."

He turned toward his desk and withdrew the gift he'd bought for her in London. Her eyes widened with surprise when he handed her the fancy package.

She gasped when she opened the box, revealing the Cartier watch he'd purchased at Harrods.

"I guess the watch thing is sort of a retirement cliché, but I thought you might like something prettier than that damn Mickey Mouse Timex you've been wearing the last eight years."

She'd joked more than a few times over the years that her cheap Walmart watch always managed to tell the same time as his fancy Rolex. The true happiness in her eyes told him he'd found the right gift.

Sally sniffled, blinking rapidly a few times before turning away. "It's beautiful. You shouldn't have spent so much, but the truth is I'm worth every penny."

He laughed at her attempt to lighten the heavy moment.

"Thank you, Lochlan. For everything," she said thickly.

She gave him another hug, and this time she held on,

whispering, "I know what you're thinking, but you're wrong about her. I *did* hire the best person for the job. Give her six months to prove herself."

Lochlan tried to pull away, but she tightened her grip.

"Promise me. Six months."

Lochlan didn't make promises lightly, and Sally knew it. If he made the vow, he was as committed to it as May's mother had been to her name.

"She's too young. Too inexperienced."

Sally released him, locking gazes with him. Her eyebrows rose in the standard "I'm waiting" mother look, which was funny coming from Sally, who'd never been married or had kids, another thing they had in common.

Lochlan had sworn off marriage and, more importantly, children, in his early twenties. He had no desire—or time—for a bunch of snotty-nosed kids running around, making a mess of his house. His life was perfect the way it was—satisfying work, a comfortable, quiet home and Sundays spent at the Collins Dorm, watching football with his family.

Lochlan had it made, and he knew it.

When he let the silence drag on too long, she said his name. "Lochlan."

"Fine," he grumbled. "Six months. Not a day longer."

"She won't need more than a week to prove herself. I only asked for that much time because you're stubborn when it comes to admitting you're wrong."

He chuckled. "*Why* am I sad you're leaving?"

She laughed, gripping his forearm. "I'd tell you to try to slow down and not work so much, but I know the advice would be wasted on you."

"It would."

"You've built something wonderful here at AdLoch, something to be proud of, but there's a lot more to life than this company, Lochlan. Make sure you remember that."

"You sound like my Pop Pop."

"If that was meant to be an insult, you failed completely. That man is the wisest person I know."

Lochlan grasped her hand and gave it a gentle squeeze. "I didn't mean it as an insult."

She smiled, pressing her lips together tightly before saying a hurried goodbye and walking out. Sally wouldn't want him to see her cry.

Hell, he was fighting some pretty powerful emotions right now too. His throat was tight, his stomach tied in knots.

From the doorway, he could see Sally giving May a quick hug as well before leaving. The door to the outer office closed and, sinking down into his leather chair, Lochlan felt as though the lid had just been closed on his coffin.

He snorted. Jesus. Melodramatic much?

Unfortunately, the self-deprecation didn't help. He'd just committed to babysitting a wet-behind-the-ears administrative assistant for the next six months.

"Would you like a cup of coffee?" May asked from the doorway. "You drink it black, right?"

He nodded. "That would be great."

She gave him a tentative smile that told him he'd done a shitty job welcoming her. Then he figured it was probably better this way. Better for her to see that he wasn't a coddler, wasn't the type to smile and say please. He wasn't exactly an asshole either. He praised efficient work, but when he asked for something, he expected it to be done correctly and in a timely manner. There was no way Sally could have taught May everything in just two weeks, so that meant he was going to have to practice patience. Something he genuinely sucked at.

Six months.

He sighed and turned in his chair to look out the windows of his twenty-third-floor corner office. The walls were floor-to-ceiling windows, the space bright, the view incredible as he stared down at the Inner Harbor. Baltimore was beautiful in the spring.

That was when the light bulb went on.

He'd promised not to fire May. Nothing was said in regards to her quitting.

He didn't plan to be unkind or unfair, but he was going to be himself. Business at AdLoch was going to go on exactly as usual.

The best plan was to show May what she was getting into, no sugarcoating or lightening the load. She would either keep up or she wouldn't. And if she couldn't, she'd quit.

The plan was perfect because it meant his life hadn't changed at all. He was going to do the job the same way he always had, expecting the same things from May that he'd asked of Sally. No patience required.

"It's a lovely view."

Lochlan watched May walk toward him through the reflection in the window, not bothering to turn around until she placed his coffee on his desk.

"It is," he agreed. He spun around and gestured to one of the chairs across from him. Time to lay the cards on the table. "Tell me about your previous work experience, May."

"I'm afraid there's not a lot to tell. I worked as a receptionist at Phelps Technology, while taking community college classes at night to earn my Administrative Assistant certification. I was promoted to that role for one of the junior partners of the ad firm. I loved the job, but there wasn't much room for continued advancement there. It's a relatively small company."

Lochlan struggled to understand why Sally saw May as the

most qualified candidate. He'd offered a lucrative salary and benefit package that would have certainly ensured his applicant pool had been large, filled with much more experienced —and even better educated—hopefuls.

What had made May stand out from the crowd?

"Are you dating anyone, engaged, married?"

May shook her head. "Only to my work."

He grinned at her smooth answer. Sally had often accused him of the same, telling him booty calls were not the same thing as relationships, and he'd be smart to figure that out before he was an old man with a bulging waist and receding hairline. "I assume Sally warned you that I'm a workaholic."

May lifted one shoulder, unwilling to betray whatever confidences Sally had shared about him as a boss. "I'm perfectly aware that I was vastly underqualified for this position, but I promise you, Mr. Wallace, I'm capable of doing the job. I'm a quick learner, a hard worker, and I won't let you down."

Lochlan felt a slight sense of déjà vu as he recalled Sally saying something similar to him at her own interview.

"I realize I'm older than most assistants, but I have the experience and the drive to do this job. You won't be sorry."

Perhaps Sally had seen shades of herself in May. If so, then maybe she *had* hired the best person for the job. Lochlan wished he could make himself believe that.

"I'm sure you won't. I apologize for my behavior earlier. I made assumptions about what Sally would look for in an assistant. That's not your fault. It's mine."

May's hands were folded in her lap, gripped together tightly.

"I will warn you that I'm not the type of man to ask for things nicely or tie them up with a please. I'm afraid that may come across as brusque or rude, but I assure you, I don't mean it that way."

"I don't need pretty words, Mr. Wallace. My job is to make yours easier. Sally gave me a list of her assigned tasks, but if there's something I'm not doing that you need, or something I'm doing wrong, I hope you'll let me know."

Her confidence belied her looks. Everything May said was professionally reassuring, but when she tucked the strand of blonde hair that had fallen from her ponytail behind her ear, he was struck by that same first impression.

Vulnerability.

There was no negating its presence. There was also no denying that May thought she was hiding it.

"Work hours are nine to five, however, there are many times when we'll need to work later into the night or even on weekends. The salary for this position is high because the hours are long. Will that be a problem for you?"

She shook her head, but he noticed the slightest hesitance before she said, "No. Not at all."

The phone rang once more and May walked to her desk to answer it.

From that point forward, the workday proceeded as always as May fielded phone calls, kept him on schedule and his coffee cup full.

Sally *had* trained her well.

While May was all business, Lochlan was anything but. He kept sneaking surreptitious peeks at her, her desk visible through the open door of his office. He pulled the file Sally had given him about May from his briefcase and read the thing from beginning to end. It corroborated May's comments about her education and experience, but told him precious little about her on a personal level.

When too much hair had escaped, May tugged out the

ponytail holder, running her fingers through her long tresses to comb it before pinning it up once more.

Lochlan didn't realize he was staring at her until she turned and caught him watching.

He flicked his eyes toward his computer and silently kicked himself for being such a jackass. He was probably coming off as creepy. He struggled to concentrate on the contract an associate had just emailed him.

At this rate, it would be May firing *him*. He was failing miserably at his job today.

"Mr. Wallace?"

May's voice called out to him from her desk.

"Yes?"

"There's a Mr. Raffi on the phone. Are you available to speak with him?"

"Of course. Put the call through."

The day seemed to last an eternity and at the end of it, he had precious little to show for the hours. Work would distract him for a few minutes to an hour, then his attention would return to May as he tried to figure her out.

By the time five o'clock rolled around, his initial concerns about May's ability to do the job were slowly fading.

However, it had been an easy day. There would be just as many that required long hours and putting out multiple fires at the same time. She hadn't truly been tested yet.

"It's quitting time," May said quietly from the doorway of his office. "Do you need me to stay late?"

He shook his head. "No. I'm still suffering some jet lag. I'm gonna call it a day too. I'll see you tomorrow?" He hadn't meant to make the statement a question, though it had come out that way.

"Yes, sir," she replied.

Lochlan's heart pounded at the soft, almost breathless way

she called him sir, his gaze glued to her face as he suddenly understood the meaning behind the vulnerability he'd sensed.

May flushed under his intense study—and bowed her head for just a second, the move so submissive, so stunning, he struggled to find his breath.

"Goodbye, Mr. Wallace."

"Good night," he replied gruffly.

She stood there a few seconds longer, and he got a sense she was composing herself. Then he watched as she retrieved her purse and keys before leaving.

Lochlan leaned back in his chair.

"Shit."

❧   2   ❧

Sally had hired a young, beautiful submissive.

Worse than that, May was obviously as inexperienced in that realm as she was on the work front.

Pushing himself up, Lochlan put his suit jacket back on and grabbed his own keys.

It didn't matter what she was or what she knew in that regard.

It *couldn't* matter.

She was his employee. Nothing more.

There was no food in his fridge, thanks to his extended trip overseas. Not that the thing was ever particularly full. He preferred eating out to cooking for one. And tonight, he knew exactly where he needed to be.

It was a short drive from his office to Pat's Pub. He grinned, happy to see Padraig behind the bar, leaning on the counter and talking to Pop Pop, Finn and Colm. Just the men he needed to talk to.

"Lochlan!" Padraig called out after spotting him first. "Welcome home."

Lochlan claimed the stool next to Colm, nodding his thanks as Padraig slid him a pint of his usual Guinness.

"Thanks. I have to admit you guys are a sight for sore eyes. It was a long trip."

His cousin Colm had a mind like a steel trap, never forgetting anything, something that served him well as a lawyer. He took a swig of beer and asked, "How was Sally's last day?"

"I forgot it was her last day," Colm's twin brother, Padraig, said. "That couldn't have been easy for you. Unless, that is, you waved yet another big raise under her nose and convinced her to stay."

"She retired."

"I like that woman," Pop Pop said. "She was good for you. And the company. But I understand her desire to move on. Life's too short to spend every year of it working."

Colm chuckled. "Says the spry ninety-two-year-old still here at the pub. How's the replacement?"

"May Flowers," Lochlan said, trying to figure out what else to add.

"Come from April showers?" Finn asked, obviously searching for a reason behind his odd comment.

Lochlan chuckled. "Her name is May Flowers."

"No way," Padraig said with a laugh. "That's kind of cool."

"Is she older like Sally?" Finn asked.

Lochlan shook his head. "Young. *Very* young." It was on the tip of his tongue to say "too young," but that wasn't really true. May was much more mature than his younger cousins who were close to the same age, but that was probably an unfair comparison. Fiona and Sunnie seemed younger than May, more carefree and a little bit sillier, but that didn't mean they were incapable of working hard and doing well in their professions. He just never saw them in that environment. Fiona had already found quite a lot of success as a sitcom writer in Hollywood, and Sunnie was about to graduate from college with a nursing degree.

"Are you not okay with Sally's choice, son?" Pop Pop asked.

"No...I mean, yes. I'm concerned about her age, but if first impressions count, I have to say she seems capable of doing the job. She ran the office just like Sally, very efficiently."

Pop Pop frowned. "Then I'm not sure I understand why you look down in the dumps right now."

Colm snickered. "I might have an idea. How hot is May?"

Lochlan released a long breath—one he thought he might have been holding all damn day. "She's fucking gorgeous."

"Language," Pop Pop murmured without anger.

"Sorry, Pop Pop."

"Hey, guys." Aunt Riley walked up to them. "Oh, Lochlan, you're back. How was London?"

"True to the cliché. Rainy and cold."

"That sucks. Listen. I'm sorry to break things up, but I've got a banging headache."

Finn turned toward his mom with concern. "Did you take some Advil?"

She nodded. "Yeah. It's kicking in, but I still think crawling into bed sounds pretty good."

"This headache wouldn't have anything to do with those margaritas you and Bubbles fell into last night to celebrate Sunnie's upcoming graduation, would they?" Pop Pop asked.

Finn rolled his eyes and laughed. "Jeez, Mom. You're hungover?"

"Blame Bubbles. She's a bad influence on me."

Every single man snorted in unison, none of them fooled by that line of bullshit. Riley and Bubbles, a former Vegas prostitute turned nurse, had been best friends for close to thirty years. If there'd been a third woman at last night's impromptu margarita party, maybe she could have claimed she was led astray, but Bubbles and Riley were nearly always the ringleaders, guiding people down wicked paths hand in hand.

Riley rolled her eyes, the action prompting a pained wince. "You're all hilarious. Do you mind if we take off early tonight, Pop? It's a bye night for the Stanley Cup, so you won't miss anything fun around here."

"What are *we*? Chopped liver?" Padraig joked.

"I think we're fun," Finn said.

Pop Pop had moved out of the apartment above the pub well over a decade earlier and now lived with Aunt Riley. He'd given up his driver's license a few years earlier, simply because he never used it. Riley did all the cooking at the pub, and this was where Pop Pop wanted to be, so he just hopped in the car with her every day she was working.

"*Och*. No problem, Riley. Might try to catch a repeat or two of *Wild Winters* on TV."

Riley groaned. "Suuuure, Pop. You're going to watch repeats," she said sarcastically. "*Or* you'll just watch yourself in the finale...again. For the seven-hundredth time."

Pop Pop chuckled as he rose from his stool, and Lochlan tried not to notice that he did it a bit slower each time he saw him.

Fiona was a writer for the sitcom *Wild Winters*, and a month earlier, they'd filmed an episode of the show in the pub. Pop Pop even had a line. Lochlan had flown out to London the next day, pushing the trip back until after the filming so he wouldn't miss it.

Pop Pop placed a hand on Lochlan's shoulder. "Sally's a good woman, a savvy one, who knows you well. I can promise you, she didn't hire May because she was pretty. Open your eyes and try to find the reason she did. Figure that out and all will be well."

"Thanks. I will."

"Catch you tomorrow night, Pop Pop," Padraig said as their grandfather and Riley headed out.

"Alright," Colm said, leaning back in the high stool. "Let's have the unabridged version, now that Pop Pop is gone."

"I can't figure out what the hell Sally was thinking in hiring May."

"Is it really the fact that she's young and pretty that's bothering you?" Finn asked. Lochlan appreciated the disbelief in his cousin's tone. He was grateful that Finn thought him above such pettiness.

Padraig flipped a towel over his shoulder, obviously sharing Finn's same sense of confidence in Lochlan's character. "She was probably thinking you're a responsible, respectful man who can be around a woman without thinking with his dick."

"Yeah," Lochlan muttered.

"That doesn't sound very reassuring." Colm was frowning.

"I walked into that office after four hours of sleep, jet-lagged, and grumpy about Sally retiring. I probably wasn't in the best frame of mind to meet her."

"What did you do?"

"Acted like a bear, questioned Sally's choice...in front of May. Then spent the rest of the day staring at her like a goddamn fool, trying to figure her out."

"Figure her out?" Finn asked.

"There was something about her, something I couldn't put my finger on."

"Like what? Like you recognized her or something?" Given Finn's confusion, it was obvious Lochlan was doing a shitty job explaining.

"No. There were these feelings—"

Finn crossed his arms and narrowed his eyes.

"Not sexual," Lochlan quickly corrected. At least...not at first. Not until she'd said goodbye, and he'd realized what it was that he kept seeing.

Lochlan and his cousins were close—like best-friends close. They may be blood, but they were also his confidantes, the guys he turned to when he needed advice or just to brag about some hot conquest.

"I'm pretty sure she's submissive."

Padraig blew out a low whistle. Finn shot him a sympathetic look.

Colm, however, went straight for the solution. "You've been gone a month. Give Adrienne a call."

"Yeah. That's probably not a bad idea."

Adrienne Walcott was Lochlan's booty call, and he was hers. Neither of them had the time for or interest in a relationship. More than that, they weren't well suited, sharing very few interests in common. However, they had one very important similarity. While they were oil and water outside the bedroom, they were a matched set *inside*, Adrienne the perfect submissive to his Dom. They'd met in a club a few years earlier, and since then, they'd taken their bedroom play away from the more public setting, meeting in hotels once every few weeks or so.

"Or better yet, go out on a real date," Padraig suggested.

Lochlan shook his head. "No thanks. I'm good with the no-strings-attached deal."

Colm snickered. "You're talking to the last of the confirmed bachelors now that Clooney's off the market, Paddy. Lochlan's a dying breed."

Lochlan drained the rest of his beer. "You're one to talk, cuz. I don't see you sliding a ring on any woman's finger."

"Just haven't found the right one. At least I'm trying. I'm not averse to dates. And not just first ones either. I've been out with Allison four times now. She's pretty cool. Unlike you, there's not a doubt in my mind I want to get married and have kids someday."

Lochlan winced. "I thought we had a rule. No one says the K word in front of me."

"I don't get it," Finn said. "You're good with kids. When Landon showed up at the family picnic last summer with his niece and nephew, you batted that beach ball around with them for the better part of an hour. They loved you."

"That was an hour of my life, Finn. The other twenty-three hours in that day were all mine, peaceful and relaxing."

"If you consider working nonstop peaceful and relaxing." Finn drained his beer and slid the empty glass to Padraig for a refill.

Colm put a hand on Lochlan's shoulder. "You do realize the Collins curse is coming for you, right?"

"That's not funny."

Colm and Lochlan started a joke at Christmas this past year that there was a curse on their family, causing them to fall head over ass in love forever. Caitlyn, Ailis and Padraig tried to convince them it was a blessing, not a curse, but they persisted, claiming it had taken all their parents down, and now it was coming for them. Fiona had been the latest to go down hard, falling for her best friend, Asher, just last month.

"In fact," Colm said, "I've got twenty bucks that says you might be the next one to fall. Gentlemen? Any takers?"

"I'll take that bet," Finn said, reaching out to shake Colm's hand. "Lochlan is too stubborn and set in his ways. I think the curse is going to wait until he's convinced he's dodged it, and then snag him in his late forties. He'll be one of those guys everyone mistakes for a grandfather at his own kid's graduation."

"K word," Lochlan warned. "And it's never going to happen."

"You want a piece of the action, Padraig?" Colm asked.

Padraig tilted his head, studying Lochlan's face. "No. I'm pretty sure you're right, Colm."

"*Et tu*, Brute?" Lochlan shook his head when Padraig picked up his empty pint glass, pointing at it to see if he wanted another.

"Tell me this, Lochlan. Is May a good assistant?" Padraig asked.

"It's only been a day, but yeah, she's seems very capable, very..." He sighed. "Sally-like. We didn't talk much, but she's smart and confident, and she's got a great smile, an easy laugh." He was digging himself into a hole, discussing things that didn't matter from an employer's perspective. Especially considering he'd just revealed his suspicions about May being submissive.

Padraig grinned, amused by his description. "Then it sounds to me like you got lucky. Sally hired the right person for the job."

"Just curious," Colm said, "how young is young?"

"Twenty-three."

"Fucking gorgeous, great laugh, and submissive, huh? Is she single?" Colm asked.

Lochlan nodded. "Why?"

"Because I'm not her boss."

"Neither am I," Finn added, hopping in on the joke.

This was why he'd come here. Lochlan needed his cousins to let him say the words aloud, then show him that this wasn't the end of the world. Hell, it wasn't even a bump in the road. He was perfectly capable of being around a woman without thinking with his dick, and he was definitely strong enough to resist the temptation of a workplace affair, no matter how beautiful, smart or submissive May was.

Padraig chuckled and shook his head. "You guys have issues."

"What about Allison?" Lochlan asked.

"Yeah," Finn added. "You're already dating someone, Colm. Besides, May is closer to my age than any of you clowns. I might drop by your office later in the week."

Lochlan knew they were joking, but the idea of Colm or Finn dating May bothered him for some reason.

"Forget it." Lochlan's response came out too much like a growl. "If May is able to do the job, I'd like to keep her in my employment until *I* retire, so I don't have to do this again. And if not, I'm still committed to six months."

"Six months?" Colm asked.

"Sally made me promise not to fire her until I gave her a real shot at the job."

"Damn," Finn muttered. "You must've really acted like an ass. I might need to stop by just to prove to her not all Collins men are jerks."

"You're not dating her," Lochlan repeated. "None of you are."

"Hmmm." Padraig scratched his chin and studied his face without saying anything.

Lochlan held his stare for a few seconds before saying, "What?"

Padraig picked up a dishcloth and started wiping the counter, glancing at the glasses of the patrons sitting near them. "Maybe you should hold off on calling Adrienne."

Lochlan frowned. "Why?"

Padraig tossed the cloth in the sink and straightened.

"Just...don't call her yet. I'm not a hundred percent sure you're seeing things clearly."

As far as answers went, that one sucked, but Padraig was already refilling glasses for a couple seated at the end of the bar.

"What the fuck did that mean?" Lochlan asked Finn and Colm.

Colm shrugged. "No idea. That brother of mine is getting more like Pop Pop every damn day. Regardless, he's got a point. It's only been one day, Lochlan. Get some sleep, and I guarantee within a day or two, the initial shock of losing Sally and meeting May will be gone, and life will be back to normal again. Then you can call Adrienne."

Lochlan nodded. He'd been right to come here. His family always knew what to say to give him perspective, to make an insurmountable problem seem small.

He grabbed some takeout and headed home feeling stronger, more like himself.

That feeling remained until he crawled into bed later that night. The second he closed his eyes, he saw her.

May.

Bent over his desk, her skirt tucked around her waist. She was looking at him over her shoulder, her blue eyes dark with desire, heavy-lidded, hungry.

He sat straight up and tried to shake the image away, but it stuck.

This wasn't going to end well.

May rubbed her eyes and tried to focus on the computer screen. She'd been Administrative Assistant to the CEO of AdLoch for two months, two days, seven hours, and—she glanced at the clock on the wall—seventeen minutes. During that time, she'd worked overtime nineteen days and pulled a midnighter twice.

The job was challenging, interesting and the answer to a prayer. She needed this job. Like lives-depended-on-it needed. Today was likely going to be another midnighter—a day when she and Lochlan called in for dinner and worked until neither of them could keep their eyes open.

Not that the long nights were horrible. The last time they'd stayed late, they'd wound up getting into a huge debate over the Lucas *Star Wars* films versus the newer ones made since Disney took ownership. Lochlan claimed the originals were the best and the franchise had been destroyed by Disney. She disagreed. They'd actually lost an hour of work time arguing about it, looking up certain scenes online, trying to convince each other to their perspective.

It had been fun, but in the end, she'd felt guilty for remaining at work when she was needed at home.

May prayed all would be well tonight. This job kept her away from home too much, and it was putting a lot of stress on her already fragile mother. The string was stretched taut, and May knew it was just a matter of time before it broke completely. Unfortunately, May didn't have a choice. They needed the money this job was bringing in—desperately.

The fact she loved working at AdLoch helped, but then... it didn't help. She enjoyed being here, which made her feel guilty because she was needed at home just as much. May was torn in two, trying to fill the large shoes left by Sally, while at the same time not letting her family down.

She was burning the candle at both ends, which actually wasn't as hard as it should be.

Because of *him*.

She was completely impressed with and in awe of her new boss, Lochlan Wallace. He was brilliant, handsome as sin, confident and rich, yet at the same time, he was approachable and real. He'd tried to warn her away at the beginning, claiming he couldn't sugarcoat his requests. In truth, she'd loved that honesty and had been relieved by it.

Her last boss had equated youth to inability. He hadn't exactly treated her like she was stupid, but there'd been a lack of trust in her intelligence, so he'd over-explained her tasks and limited what she was assigned. Every hour there had felt like five years.

AdLoch was the opposite. She was busy from open to close. Lochlan had handed her all of Sally's roles and trusted that she could follow through. She was exhausted yet exhilarated, and the challenge fulfilled her like nothing she'd ever done.

The only downside to her new job was something that wasn't Lochlan's fault, something he would probably be mortified to hear, so she was careful to hide it.

Lochlan had a way of looking at her that had her imagining things that never occurred to her before...sexually explicit, kinky-as-hell things.

Even though she typically dropped onto the couch each night, tired beyond belief, the second she closed her eyes, he was there, tying her up, spanking her, pulling her hair, taking her over and over, hard and fast and glorious.

"May."

She jerked at the sound of Lochlan's voice next to her. She hadn't heard him approaching.

She flushed, her cheeks heating under his intense gaze. "Yes, sir?"

She had no idea why saying those words impacted her so... roughly. It was a common enough thing to say to a boss. Perhaps it was his response to them. His eyes narrowed for just a moment, not in anger, but with some other emotion she couldn't put her finger on. She thought it might be desire...or something more primal.

God, she really needed to get a handle on this.

May found it difficult to breathe when he was nearby. She licked her suddenly dry lips, scraping the lower one with her teeth, biting it nervously. His gaze followed the movement.

The first few weeks, she'd chalked up this damp-palms, light-headed feeling to nervousness, until she realized Lochlan didn't frighten her at all. He turned her on.

"Do you have the Hilty file? I can't find it anywhere."

She nodded, forcing her eyes away to sift through a pile of folders on her desk. "I took it to make copies of the notes

Sally made about the deal. I'm sorry I didn't put it back afterwards."

May held the file out. His fingers brushed hers as he reached for it.

"No harm, no foul," he said with a smile. "You good to stay a little late tonight?"

Given the fact it was nearly five thirty and at least eighty percent of the employees had already called it day, she figured that was obvious.

She nodded. "Sure." She would have to call her mother and run through the nightly routine for her. May had anticipated this, so she'd prepared a meal, something her mom would only have to heat up.

"Would you like more coffee?" she asked.

"No thanks. Thought I might grab a bottle of water from the mini-fridge in my office. Want one?"

She shook her head and pointed to the half-drunk water on her desk. "I'm fine."

"You know, I've been meaning to talk to you."

May drew in a slow breath. "Is everything okay?"

He held his hand up to ward off her concern. "Everything is great. That's what I wanted to say. You're doing a wonderful job, May. I hope you're happy here. I know the hours are long, but—"

"I'm very happy. The work is much more challenging than my previous job, which was pretty boring."

He grinned.

"Okay. It was a lot boring. Every day at AdLoch brings something new. And all the people who work here are really nice."

"I've heard the same said of you."

May was relieved to hear that. Part of her duties as Lochlan's admin assistant included handling employees. Sally had warned her that as the company grew, she'd sort of assumed the role of HR naturally. Apparently, the older woman and Lochlan had discussed taking those tasks out of the job description for the new hire, but decided against it. Lochlan preferred having his "finger on the pulse of the office," as Sally had explained. So she—and now May—dealt with employee issues, keeping Lochlan in the loop.

Fortunately, there hadn't been much in the way of workplace drama yet. AdLoch rented out this entire floor of the high-rise, complete with a whole bank of offices lining the outside walls, as well as a larger, more open space in the middle that consisted of a long conference table, break room and about a dozen cubicles for lower-level employees. She and Lochlan worked in the large corner suite, but she spent a great deal of time out in the common area as well, communicating Lochlan's directives, requesting information, and setting up meetings between her boss and the different departments.

Lochlan was a tech genius, and he'd certainly built something pretty wonderful. May was delighted to be a part of it.

Her cell phone rang. At her last job, she kept her personal cell turned off and stashed in her drawer. She'd done the same here for the first couple of weeks, but as her hours increased, so did her anxiety about home.

"I thought I turned that off," she lied. May reached for it, intending to silence the thing, until she saw the number on the screen. "I'm so sorry. I have to take this."

She kept her eyes averted, praying Lochlan wouldn't be annoyed by her receiving personal calls at work. "Hello?" She paused. "This is she."

Lochlan remained by her desk. She felt him standing there, nearby, as she listened to the 911 operator, her heart racing with fear as the woman told her about the fire in the kitchen of her apartment.

Apparently the fire was out, but police and firefighters were still there with her family. Her mother was distressed, according to the operator, so they'd called her.

"Is everyone okay?"

"What is it?" Lochlan murmured.

May looked up at him. "Fire," she whispered as the operator said the police weren't comfortable leaving her mother alone. "I understand. I'm leaving work right now. I'll be there in ten minutes." Ordinarily, she walked to and from work, the trip taking half an hour or so. This time she'd have to get an Uber. "Thank you for calling."

She hung up and looked at Lochlan. They had a huge meeting with a client at ten a.m. tomorrow. The timing on this sucked.

"Mr. Wallace—" she started.

"Grab your bag, May. I texted the valet to bring my car around the second you said 'fire.'"

"That's okay. I can call a cab."

Lochlan crossed his arms. "Get your bag."

It was clear he wouldn't take no for an answer, so she did as he said, retrieving her purse and her keys. Her hands were shaking despite her efforts to remain calm.

Lochlan took her empty hand in his large palm and gave it a reassuring squeeze. "Who was that on the phone?"

"A 911 operator."

"And what did they say?"

"There was a small fire in my kitchen. It's out now, but my mother..." May swallowed, her throat clogged with fear.

"You and your mother live together?"

May nodded. She had been very careful not to bring her situation at home to work. Sally knew about it, but May had asked the woman not to tell Lochlan. Her personal life was just that—personal. It was important to her to maintain professionalism at work at all times.

Not that Lochlan hadn't tried to discover more about her life. He'd asked questions occasionally, but she was very good at vague answers. Lately, he had stopped asking.

"I know you have a lot to do to prepare for tomorrow's meeting. I can just...go home and...make sure everything is okay and come right back. You don't have to come with—"

Lochlan was still holding her hand, and he used that grip to guide her toward the exit. He obviously had no intention of changing his mind about driving her by the time they reached the car and he opened the passenger door. If she weren't on the cusp of a mini freak-out, she would have appreciated how sweet his Audi was.

He climbed behind the wheel. "What's the address?"

She gave it to him, and she didn't miss the slight frown that crossed his face. "You walk to work every day?"

May nodded, perfectly aware of what he was thinking. Her apartment was a fair distance from the office, and the neighborhood wasn't exactly the best. Baltimore was one of those places where one block too far would take you from affluent to scary-as-fuck before you realized what had happened. She lived just on the border of scary.

"And on the nights we work late?"

May looked out the passenger side window as she lied. "I grab a cab." She didn't look back at him, pretending to be fascinated by the city streets.

She let the silence drag out another few minutes before chancing a peek over. Lochlan was staring straight ahead— and he looked pissed off. Had he realized her words were a lie? How could he?

May understood how dangerous it was to walk alone at

night, but even with the nice pay raise, she didn't have enough money to waste on cab fare. At least not yet.

Lochlan pulled up in front of her apartment building, claiming one of the spots vacated by a departing fire truck. There were still two police cars and an ambulance parked outside.

"Thank you for the ride," she said. "I'll try to get back to work as soon as I can."

She hoped he would take the hint. The last thing on earth she wanted was for him to follow her inside.

When he opened the car door and stepped out, she realized she wasn't going to get her wish.

"Mr. Wallace—" she started. She was anxious to get upstairs, but she was just as determined to keep him out.

"Lochlan."

"What?"

"I want you to start calling me Lochlan."

She shook her head. "I don't think that's..." It was on the tip of her tongue to tell him that wasn't a good idea. Lochlan felt too personal, too close. Instead, she said, "Professional."

"It is if I say it is. I'm the boss." He gestured toward the front door of her building, his scowl growing darker when she opened the door without a key. "No security?"

"There's a system, but it's been down a few months. The landlord said he's waiting on a part or something."

May was perfectly aware that line from her dick of a landlord was bullshit, but given the murderous look on Lochlan's face, she thought it best to give him some answer that might calm him down.

They walked up three flights of stairs to get to her place. May usually didn't see the dinginess of the place, used to the ratty carpet, the broken elevator, the loose stairs along the way. As she rushed up, her eyes took in everything, imagining what Lochlan must be thinking as he followed.

When they reached her floor, the door was open and she could hear the raised voice of her landlord, smell the lingering stench of smoke.

"Shit," she murmured. Jenks Peterson was an asshole on a good day.

She turned, intent on making one last ditch effort to send Lochlan back to the office.

She only managed to say, "Listen, I think..." before he walked by her and inside the apartment.

"Aunt May!" Little Chloe launched herself across the room, wrapping her arms around her legs. "The kitchen was on fire."

"I heard. Are you okay, sweetie?"

Chloe nodded, and May let her gaze travel around the room. Her mother was sitting quietly on the couch, wringing her hands.

"I'm so sorry, May. I turned on the wrong burner, and the towel..." Her mother's words faded away as May gently extracted herself from Chloe's iron-tight grip so she could get to the couch.

She dropped down next to her mom and took her hands in hers. "It's okay. It was an accident. Where's Jenny?" she asked as she looked around the room, sighing with relief when she spotted her other niece standing in the corner, silent as ever. "You okay, Jen?" she called out across the room.

Jenny simply held her gaze, offering neither a nod or headshake. Hell, May wouldn't mind if her mute niece flipped her the middle finger. At least it would be some sign of life.

"You're going to have to pay to repair that kitchen," the landlord said. "And it won't be cheap."

May stood and walked toward the kitchen, dreading what she was going to see.

It was pretty much exactly what she'd feared. The stove was a total loss, as was the counter next to it. One whole wall was charred, the linoleum on that side of the floor destroyed. The ceiling and the rest of the room were severely smoke damaged. They'd most likely have to gut the whole room and start over.

"I have renter's insurance," she said, not bothering to mention the high premium. May was going to have to adjust the timeline on her plans to move the four of them out of this dump. Six months to a new life now looked more like a year.

"I have connections to a construction firm," Lochlan said. "I'll place a call."

May nodded, numbness covering her like a blanket. The past few years had been a constant roller coaster of emotions. So much so, she'd lost the ability to cry or rage.

"I have an approved list of people who can work in the building," Jenks said belligerently.

"I'm sure you do. I'll send you the information on my firm first thing in the morning. They're one of the top five companies in the state. I doubt you'll have an issue with them. And since May will be the one paying, the choice should be hers."

Jenks narrowed his eyes. May was aware of the landlord's "approved list." It consisted primarily of his buddies who overinflated their prices, laughing all the way to the bank on the backs of the renters in the building.

May had always known Jenks was a blowhard and a bully, but his response to Lochlan's presence merely confirmed it. "I'll send *you* the approved list," he repeated to May, ignoring Lochlan completely.

She gestured with a tilt of her head toward Lochlan. "I think I'd like his guys to do the work."

"Ms. Flowers—" Jenks started.

"Then it's settled. Is there anything else you need?" Lochlan's tone was stern, dismissive.

Jenks was used to being the boss in the apartment building. He spoke, and he expected others to listen, so he clearly felt the need to exert his power in the face of Lochlan's dominance. "One more problem in this apartment, May, and that's it. You're out."

Lochlan took one step forward, the movement putting him in front of May, forming a wall between her and the swarthy landlord. She'd always acknowledged his size—Lochlan was built like a mountain, tall and wide—but she had never seen him use that height for intimidation. Right now, he was, and it was seriously impressive.

"I'd rethink that threat. Try to evict her over an accident and I'll have the housing commission in here tomorrow. I saw several code violations just on the walk up here."

Jenks took a step back, peering at her from around Lochlan. "We'll talk tomorrow, May."

The landlord realized he wouldn't win tonight, not with Lochlan in the room. Which meant he'd give her twice the earful in the morning. So Jenks, the EMTs, and the two remaining police officers left, closing the door behind them, and drawing her attention back to the strong smell of smoke still lingering in the apartment.

Her mother sighed. "I really don't like that landlord."

"Mr. Wallace, this is my mom, Linda Flowers."

Lochlan shook her hand. "Nice to meet you, Linda."

"And you. I think I'm going to go back to my room and lie down, May."

"That's fine, Mom. I'm here. I'll take care of everything."

Her mother walked down the hall slowly, and May watched until she entered her room and shut the door.

May turned toward her nieces. "Why don't the two of you grab sweaters from your room? We'll have to go out for dinner tonight."

Chloe danced down the hall, clearly excited about the upcoming Happy Meal. Jenny—as usual—slunk away soundlessly. Lochlan watched them leave with great interest.

"Thank you for helping me deal with Jenks, Mr. Wallace. He's—"

"Lochlan."

May sighed when he corrected her. "I told you I didn't—"

"I know. Now say it."

"Mr.—"

Lochlan placed one finger under her chin, drawing her eyes to his face. "Try again."

He was barely touching her, but May felt as though she'd just received two-thousand volts. "Please," she said. "I think we need to maintain...I mean..."

Lochlan bent his head closer, holding eye contact. The man must have been a snake charmer in another life. She was hypnotized, paralyzed. "Say it, May."

"Lochlan," she whispered.

He smiled, his light touch gone.

It took everything she had not to feel her chin to see if it was singed.

"My uncle Killian and his partner, Justin, own a construction firm. My uncle Sean works there as well. They can fix your kitchen up quickly and efficiently, and they won't fleece you. I'm fairly certain the same can't be said of your landlord."

"You're right about that. I appreciate you passing on the name."

"Let me know if Jenks gives you any more trouble."

There was no way in hell May would do that. She fought her own battles, and she'd already crossed too many lines tonight, bringing him into her home, calling him by his first name, letting him see...her life.

May glanced around the room and winced. The place was a mess, and while she wanted to blame the overabundance of firefighters and police tromping through, the truth was, it hadn't looked that much better when she'd left for work today. May prided herself on keeping a clean apartment, but since starting at AdLoch, she hadn't been here enough to keep it up to her standards. She'd tried to give the girls a list of chores, but her mother didn't enforce it, so too many things had fallen to the wayside.

"Your mother and nieces live with you?"

May nodded.

Lochlan's gaze traveled around the apartment, down the hallway. "Two-bedroom place?"

Damn. The observant man had even counted the doors.

She nodded again, deciding she could keep answering yes or no questions, or just do the full disclosure now and get it over with. "Yes. It was just me and my mom until six months ago. My brother and his wife were killed in a car accident, so the girls came to live with us. I gave them my bedroom, and until we can afford to get a bigger place, I just sleep out here."

Lochlan looked around the room. "You sleep out here? On the couch?"

"I realize it's not exactly ideal, but we're making it work. It was one of the reasons I applied for the job as your admin assistant. The pay increase. Listen, I know I said I would take care of things here and return to the office later, but this could take a little while."

Lochlan snorted. "Neither one of us is going back to work tonight."

"I don't want to keep you from preparing for—"

"I'm not leaving you alone in the midst of all this."

May looked around. Apart from the smell of smoke, this was pretty much as good as her life got.

Regardless, his desire to help struck a chord deep inside. God, it almost made her want to step into his arms and sob like a baby.

She swallowed the emotion down. "I'm fine. Honest."

Lochlan had a bad habit of ignoring her when she didn't agree with him. "Grab the girls and your mother. I'm taking you all out to dinner. I know a place I think you'll like."

She shook her head. One of them needed to be practical. "But you have the big meeting with Charles Durwood tomorrow."

"I've been in this business enough years to know what I'm doing, May. Don't worry about it. I've laid most of the groundwork with Charles. Tomorrow, I just drive it all home."

It was more than that, and May—even in her two short months of employment—knew it. "You've already gone above and beyond tonight. I don't expect you to feed us as well."

Lochlan pointed down the hall. Chloe and Jenny were heading toward them. "Go get your mom."

May stopped fighting and did as he said. She peeked her head into her mother's room, unsurprised to find her in her nightgown in bed, happily watching her favorite game show. "We're heading out for some dinner. Want to come?"

Mom shook her head. "No, dear. I'm a bit tired."

"Okay. We'll bring you something back."

"That would be fine, dear. That man with you...that's your new boss?"

"Yeah."

Mom smiled. "He looks nice."

"He is. We'll be back soon."

Mom waved. "I'll be here."

May returned to the living room. "She's going to stay in, so I guess it's just the four of us."

As they walked down several flights of stairs, Chloe rained down a million and twelve questions on poor Lochlan. She was inquisitive, tireless, and smart. May adored her energy, but she'd gotten more than a few emails from her first-grade teacher about Chloe losing her daily behavior stars due to constant talking or for getting out of her chair without permission to chat with her best friend.

May actually preferred those emails, as opposed to the ones from Jenny's teacher. Jenny hadn't spoken a word since her parents' death. The guidance counselor at the school was trying to work with Jenny, claiming the young girl's self-inflicted mutism was a serious problem, one that required real therapy with a psychologist.

May agreed, and had even called a few, but the hard truth was, they simply didn't have the money to pay for it.

"Where are we going to eat?" Chloe asked as they climbed into Lochlan's car.

So far, bless him, Lochlan had answered every single question patiently, looking somewhat amused. "My family owns an Irish restaurant."

The sweet girl made a face. "What's Irish?"

"Ireland is a country on the other side of the Atlantic Ocean, and the people who live there are Irish."

"What do they eat?" Chloe asked.

"Chloe, baby. I think you've asked poor Mr. Wallace enough questions."

Lochlan glanced over as they stopped at a light. "Lochlan. And I don't mind her questions. You never learn anything if you don't ask." For the remainder of the ride to the restaurant, Lochlan described Irish fare, proclaiming his aunt made the best bangers and mash in Baltimore.

Chloe giggled at the name, telling him bangers was a silly way to say sausage. He agreed with her.

As they passed through the front door of Sunday's Side—the restaurant attached to his family's Irish pub—May was assaulted by the delicious smells, her mouth watering, her stomach growling loudly.

Lochlan chuckled at the sound.

She shrugged good-naturedly. "Lunch was a long time ago."

"You're right. It was." He directed them toward a booth. Chloe darted ahead of May, sliding in next to Jenny. Lochlan waited for her to slide in, then claimed the rest of the space next to her. Their close proximity reminded her of his size once more.

An attractive older woman approached the table. "What do we have here? A dinner party?"

Lochlan grinned. "Hi, Mom. Couldn't get to the table any quicker?"

Lochlan's mother laughed softly. "I wanted to at least give you time to sit down. Besides, you have to admit, Lochlan. This isn't your usual crowd."

"Mom, this is May Flowers and her nieces, Jenny and Chloe. May, this is my mother, Keira Wallace."

Recognition dawned on his mother's face as she reached out to shake May's hand. "Of course, you took Sally's place, you poor thing. How is my son treating you? Working you to death?"

"Mother," Lochlan murmured in a low voice.

May laughed. "He's an absolute slave driver. Keeps me toiling from dawn to midnight with only occasional breaks for bread and water."

Chloe, too young to get the joke, tilted her head in confusion. "That's not what you said at home. You told Nana he was really nice and not hard to look at. But I don't know what that means. Looking at people isn't hard."

May felt heat rise to her cheeks as Lochlan and Keira laughed.

"Out of the mouths of babes," Keira said.

Lochlan wiggled his eyebrows at May. "You think I'm hot?"

"This is an inappropriate conversation, Mr. Wallace."

Lochlan's body stilled, and she realized he was hell-bent on her calling him by his first name.

Keira saved her, glancing at the girls. "And how old are you two?"

"I'm six," Chloe said, pointing to Jenny. "She's eight. She doesn't talk anymore."

"Anymore?" Keira asked.

Lochlan's gaze drifted toward Jenny as well. May could imagine him replaying the night so far, recalling Jenny's silence. She searched for some way to explain the comment without hurting her young niece.

Chloe, however, was too quick. "Since our mommy and daddy died."

Jenny's expression never changed. The girl was locked down tighter than a vault.

"I see." Keira's eyes softened and, bless the woman, she guided the conversation away to something less painful. "And the two of you live with your aunt May?"

Chloe nodded. "And our nana. She left a towel on the stove and nearly burned the kitchen down tonight. She called 911 while Jenny tried to put the fire out with the fire extinguisher under the sink."

That was news to May. "You did?"

Jenny didn't even look in May's direction, so she turned to Chloe for the answer. Chloe had become far too accustomed to speaking for her sister the past few months. She did so without the same pause or expectation that Jenny would speak up, as she had at the beginning. "Yeah. That tall fireman said she probably saved the whole apartment."

"I didn't know that." May reached across, intent on touching Jenny's hand. The girl anticipated her movement and slid her hands beneath the table. May swallowed down the slight. "That was incredibly smart and brave of you, Jenny."

"It was," Lochlan agreed.

Jenny's eyes darted in his direction after he spoke, just for a split second, before staring at her lap again.

"So the apartment is okay?" Keira asked.

May nodded. "The kitchen has seen better days, but we were lucky it wasn't worse. We'll be fine."

"Well, it sounds like you've had an exciting night. Here are the menus. I'm sure it won't take Yvonne very long to get over here to take your orders. She and Riley have been sneaking peeks out here ever since you walked in with two kids in tow, Lochlan."

May wasn't sure what was so fascinating about that, but she didn't question it.

Keira looked at her once more. "It was very nice to meet you, May. I hope we'll see you and your sweet nieces here again."

Lochlan took a few minutes to explain to Chloe what her options were on the menu. May tried to focus as well, but her attention kept drifting to Jenny.

The waitress, Lochlan's cousin Yvonne, appeared and was introduced as well.

Chloe placed her order, telling Yvonne to bring the same for Jenny, who, of course, offered no complaint.

When it was clear May hadn't even looked at the menu,

Lochlan leaned toward her. "Trust me to pick something for you?"

She nodded, relieved. The shock of the evening was starting to wear off, visions of her kitchen engulfed in flames, little Jenny fighting to extinguish it, her mother on the phone with 911. She could have lost everything.

And everyone.

Lochlan placed the order and reached for her menu to hand to Yvonne. May's hands were shaking again. She really needed to find a way to control that.

"Hey, Yvonne. I think Chloe and Jenny would love to meet Riley and see the kitchen. You mind giving them a quick tour?"

Yvonne was clearly surprised by the request, but she didn't question it. Instead, she gestured toward the back. "Absolutely. Aunt Riley has a million questions for these two," she said, though May couldn't imagine why. "You girls game for the tour?"

Chloe hopped out of the booth excitedly, and Jenny followed.

Lochlan took her trembling hands in his. "May. Look at me."

She did as he said, aware that her breathing was growing shallow. She was no stranger to panic attacks, but they always came in the middle of the night, when she was alone, when there was no one to see her freaking out.

She couldn't do this here.

"I'm fine," she said, willing the words to be true, repeating them in her head like a mantra. She lowered her eyes when Lochlan frowned. He wasn't fooled.

"Look at me," he repeated.

She forced her eyes back to his.

"Say my name."

His request caught her off guard. In her head, he was always Lochlan, but she knew it was much wiser to keep their boxes well-defined and limited to the workplace. He was the boss. She was his employee.

The problem was, he'd come into her home, met her family, seen too many of her struggles. He was a decent guy. He wanted to help. Right now was a perfect example of that.

But she couldn't accept it, couldn't lean on him. She'd taught herself how to manage the day to day, how to deal with all the stress—Jenny's silence, the shitty apartment, the long work hours, the lack of money, her mother's...

May pushed that thought away, refusing to finish it. She tugged her hands away and straightened her back, taking in a deep, full breath of air. It helped her ground herself again.

"I'm fine," she said softly, mostly to herself.

He studied her face.

Dammit. She hadn't meant to say that aloud again.

"I can see that."

For a moment, she thought perhaps he was speaking sarcastically. His expression changed her mind. He looked...curious.

"Jenny doesn't speak at all?"

May closed her eyes, wishing they could go back to this morning when Lochlan only saw her as his assistant. The woman with nothing more pressing or important in her life than making his coffee, setting up his schedule, and dealing with the mail.

"May?" he pressed.

"Not since her parents died. Not a word. The guidance counselor at her school has been trying to work with her, but the woman's time is extremely limited, and Jenny..."

"My aunt Lauren is a counselor. Would you be willing to let her see Jenny?"

"How big *is* your family?" She hadn't meant the question as a joke, but Lochlan took it as such, laughing loudly.

"Huge."

"I appreciate the offer, but..." May was treading on thin ice here. Lochlan was her boss. Her *new* boss. She didn't want him to think she was complaining. "I haven't quite worked out health insurance for the girls yet. They'd been on my brother's, but obviously," she took a deep breath and plowed through the rest quickly, "that ended after his death. I'm still waiting for the paperwork to clear through the courts to name me legal guardian. My brother didn't have a will or anything and nothing in the judicial system ever moves quickly. After that, I'll figure out the insurance."

"Once that clears, they'll be on your insurance from AdLoch. But that doesn't matter in this instance. Lauren won't charge you."

Her eyes widened. It was too big a favor. He'd already offered his family to help with the kitchen repairs. Now this.

She shook her head. "I couldn't ask her to do that. She doesn't know me from Adam."

"She knows *me*. She'll want to meet your niece, want to talk to her. I know Lauren. She's amazing with kids. Please consider it. After all, it's not for you. It's for Jenny."

May narrowed her eyes. "You fight dirty."

Lochlan's smile was too charming. "How do you think I made my first million?"

"Just the first million?"

"I play to win...in case you haven't noticed."

"I noticed," she said, just as Yvonne returned to the table with the girls.

Both of them were eating big dinner rolls dripping with butter.

"What about your supper?" May asked as they sat down.

"Riley told us fighting fires was hungry work and gave us a roll," Chloe explained.

May grinned. "Now *you* were fighting the fire?"

"I helped." Obviously, Chloe's tale of the night's adventure was getting bigger with each retelling, but May didn't mind. Especially when Chloe took over the majority of the conversation during the meal, entertaining them with all the drama in her first-grade classroom. Lochlan seemed enthralled by it, asking questions and commenting.

By the time the meal ended, May felt stronger, better able to deal with things again.

Lochlan drove them home and insisted on walking them upstairs.

"Okay," May said as they entered the apartment, handing the take-out bag to Chloe. "Take this to Nana, kiss her good night, and then get ready for bed. I'll be there to tuck you in after I say good night to Mr. Wallace."

Chloe skipped down the hall, Jenny following behind.

There was still a distinct smell of smoke in the room, and May wondered how long it would take to air the place out. It was starting to give her a headache.

She and Lochlan stood next to the door. "I can't thank you enough for everything you did tonight."

"I did very little, May."

She didn't think that was true at all. It had been years since anyone had extended a hand to her in kindness. Of course, when she considered that, she realized it was because she was too proud to ask for help.

"Tomorrow will be business as usual, I promise. Barring any more kitchen blazes," she joked.

Lochlan didn't laugh. He didn't even crack a smile. "I'll call my uncles about the kitchen repairs first thing in the morning. And I'll give you Lauren's number for Jenny."

She nodded, perfectly aware that even if she assured him that wasn't necessary, both things would still happen. "Thank you."

"So, we have one more thing to accomplish tonight, and then I'll leave."

May frowned. "What thing?"

"Say 'Lochlan.' You did it once, but reverted back to that damn Mr. Wallace. Clearly you need to practice."

Her shoulders slumped. The man hadn't lied when he said he played to win. She blew out a frustrated breath but said nothing.

He persisted. "Sally always called me Lochlan."

"That's different."

"How?"

"She was older, the two of you had worked together for years, and she—" Shit. May had nearly finished that sentence with *she wasn't attracted to you.*

For a second, she thought perhaps she *had* said it. Or that Lochlan could read her mind because his eyes drifted to her lips...and she got the impression the attraction wasn't one-sided.

She dismissed the idea. Her life was a mess and Lochlan had just gotten the grand tour. Her baggage had baggage. More likely, he just felt sorry for her.

"I'm not leaving until you say my name again."

She shook her head, laughing at his persistence. "Part of me is compelled to teach you a lesson in accepting the word 'no' with good grace by making you stand there all night."

He crossed his arms and, once again, she felt his size and strength. It was odd how he could increase his presence with just a look or that dominating stance.

When he didn't speak, she felt the urge to fill the silence, to give him what he wanted...to please him.

Weary beyond words, she worried what she'd do if he didn't leave soon. "Fine. Good night, Lochlan."

"I like the sound of that. It's getting better. We'll keep practicing tomorrow. Good night, May." His voice was deep and rich with a sexy rumble to it.

Lochlan left and she locked the dead bolt behind her. Something told her he'd paused in the hall to listen for that sound.

The girls were waiting for her in their bedroom, but she needed a moment to compose herself. She dropped down on the couch, staring into space, feeling completely unnerved.

"You can't lose control," she whispered to herself. "Don't start wanting things you can't have."

Her life only worked if she maintained control, if she kept the status quo, putting one foot in front of the other in an attempt to make it to the end of every day without chaos descending.

Today had been chaos.

Tomorrow, she would get them all back on track.

She didn't have any other option.

❦ 4 ❧

L ochlan was at the office early. Not that that was an unusual occurrence. He was typically the first one in. What was strange was that he hadn't fired up his computer two seconds after sitting down at his desk.

Instead, he leaned back in his chair and waited for the outer office door to open, for May to arrive.

Seeing May's home life a few days earlier had thrown him for a loop, rattled his world with such force, he was struggling to find his footing.

Lochlan prided himself on his well-ordered life. He'd put everything exactly where he wanted it—work, home, family, sex. Put it all in neat little boxes, organized, prioritized.

Work trumped everything...except his family. Pop Pop and his parents had instilled a serious work ethic in him, but they'd also driven home the belief that family was the most important thing.

He figured that was why he was still chugging along in this field when so many of his contemporaries had burned out. He took time on the weekends to spend with his family either down in the pub or up in the Collins Dorm.

Unlike the majority of his cousins, he'd opted to merely visit the family's apartment above the pub from time to time rather than live there. He preferred solitude to a large crowd of people and with each passing year, he got more set in his ways. He'd bought the perfect home, a condo near the pub and on the waterfront, that suited his needs. It was large, quiet, comfortable and his...alone.

As for sex, he knew where to go, who to turn to, to have his physical urges satisfied. Not that he'd taken advantage of that since returning from London. He'd picked up the phone to call Adrienne at least a dozen times since returning to the States. Every single time, he'd hung up before dialing the number.

What was more unusual was he hadn't answered her calls either. He wasn't sure why, but every time her name flashed on his screen, he sent her to voice mail.

He hadn't shared that information with Colm or Padraig or Finn. Partly because he was afraid they would read something into it. Something he still wouldn't let himself consider too hard.

All of those aspects of his life—work, family, home, sex— were disconnected parts that made up the whole. It worked that way.

Then he'd followed May into her shitty little apartment three nights ago, and everything about his life suddenly felt...wrong.

Empty.

He felt guilty for ever thinking May was too young and inexperienced to do the job, especially when he saw what she was dealing with at home. He'd been hard on her, right from the start, thrusting her into Sally's role without giving her time to adjust. The word *bastard* kept drifting through his mind as he recalled seeing dark circles under her eyes during her first few weeks here, thinking she'd come to her senses and realize she wasn't able to do the job, that she'd quit.

He'd been an asshole, placing the same demands on her that he'd made of Sally, and May had proven herself capable.

What bothered him the most was the understanding that this job was vital to her and her family. It was keeping a roof over their heads, food on the table.

Seeing her life, understanding what she was working for, how much she sacrificed for her family, was humbling indeed.

He felt an overpowering need to... God, to what?

To help her, to shoulder her burdens, to take control.

To be her warrior.

He wasn't sure where that last thought came from. Probably Pop Pop. The man had made a habit of reminding him what his name meant from the time he was just a kid, and how Lochlan should live up to it. He'd planted a seed, and for the first time in his life, Lochlan was starting to recognize what his grandfather meant.

The problem was, it didn't matter if he tried to help her. May wouldn't allow him to do any of that. He'd watched her waver several times over the course of the past few days. Every single time, she pulled herself back together, taking those deep breaths and muttering "I'm fine" to herself.

Her strength was immense. But Lochlan knew that at some point, it wasn't going to be enough.

His thoughts were interrupted by the sound of the door opening. His gaze drifted to the clock on the wall. Nine o'clock on the dot. May was the picture of punctuality.

He listened as she crossed the room, hanging her coat up in a small closet by the door. Then she came into view.

Her hair was pinned back in her usual neat, efficient style. He'd originally thought she wore it that way because it was quick and easy. Now he suspected it was based on her need to be taken seriously, not dismissed as too young or inexperienced.

He wanted to see it down, hanging loose over her shoulders.

She tucked her purse in her desk drawer, then disappeared again. This time, he could hear her making coffee. He still didn't bother to turn on his computer. Instead, he waited.

A few minutes later, she appeared in his doorway, his favorite mug in one hand, a sheet of paper in the other.

She smiled pleasantly as she crossed the room. "Good morning, Mr. Wallace." She placed the coffee on his desk, then took her usual seat. "You have a busy schedule today, I'm afraid."

He studied her face. May looked tired. There were dark circles under her eyes again, and they actually appeared a bit puffy, though she'd tried to conceal that fact with makeup. No doubt sleeping in the smoky apartment the past few nights had bothered them. "Sleep okay?"

"Fine." She glanced up and paused. "Is your computer not working?"

"It's working."

May studied his desk. Every file was closed. He remained in his chair, leaning back, his hands folded in front of him.

"Have you decided to work out of the office today?"

"No. I'll be here all day."

She snuck another surreptitious peek at the computer. "Okay. As you know, Mr. Durwood and his people will be here at ten to go over the contracts."

He'd won the Durwood bid. The man's business would

bring in a fair penny and set AdLoch up for its most profitable year ever.

Regardless, that win wasn't the one that mattered.

"You called me Mr. Wallace."

May sighed. "I feel very strongly about maintaining a certain level of professionalism at work. I want to thank you again for everything you did the other night, but I can assure you, from this point on, I can handle—"

"My uncle Killian called this morning. He's going to send my uncle Sean out to your place this afternoon to see what needs to be done."

"I looked up your uncle's company. I don't get the feeling they do small jobs like the repairs on my apartment."

Lochlan ignored her comment. May was digging her heels in. She had no idea what she was up against. "I told him we'd meet him there at three."

"We?"

"Yes. And Lauren is anxious to meet Jenny. She said you haven't called her yet."

"I don't feel right asking her. I would want to pay."

Lochlan continued as if she hadn't spoken. "She had an opening for an appointment for next Thursday at four. I assumed that would work, as Jenny should be out of school by then, so I told her you'd take it."

"I work until five."

He grinned at her contrary reply, his suspicions about her confirmed. May didn't have anyone to help her, so she didn't have a clue how to accept assistance when offered. "You can leave early."

"No."

"Yes."

She frowned. "I don't want you to think that I don't appreciate everything you're doing, but it's too much."

Lochlan crossed his arms. "I beg to differ." He lifted his finger when she started to speak again. "And nothing I've just said to you is negotiable. Period. Now," he turned to fire up his computer, "as you said, Durwood will be here soon, so let's take the next hour to make sure we have everything we need for the ten o'clock meeting."

May looked like she wanted to argue, but she didn't. He knew she felt enough guilt about leaving work to deal with the fire that she would yield. He also knew he was in good shape for the meeting, something that became apparent to May about thirty minutes after they'd started setting things up.

She accompanied him to the meeting, taking notes, which went just as well as he'd anticipated.

May ate lunch at her desk, typing up the meeting summary, and he spent the better part of the afternoon with his lawyer, discussing the contracts.

However, Lochlan kept an eye on the clock, aware that they would need to leave here by two forty-five in order to meet Uncle Sean at her apartment.

"May, can you run this report..." He stopped speaking when he looked up and realized May wasn't at her desk. Lochlan stood, his muscles stiff from sitting so long, and decided he'd deliver the report to the CFO's office. The short walk would do him good.

He was halfway through the large central office space when he heard May's voice.

"I'm fairly certain Mr. Wallace wouldn't approve of you organizing a betting pool if you didn't include him, Tom."

He chuckled, ducking behind a cubicle so she wouldn't know he was there. Lochlan was a Collins, through and through, which meant there weren't too many bets he wouldn't take. May had figured that out quickly.

"Hey, May," Trixie Watkins called out. "Here's that birthday card for Ronald. I got everyone in my department to sign it."

"Terrific. I think you guys were the last ones. The cake will be delivered tomorrow at lunchtime."

"Chocolate?" Trixie asked.

"Is there any other kind?" May replied with a light laugh.

Another voice entered the conversation. "Hey, did Lochlan have a chance to look at that report I sent over yesterday?"

"Not yet, Bill. He was wrapped up all morning with the Durwood contracts. It's the next thing on his to-do list. I promise I'll make sure he gets to it today."

"Thanks, May."

Lochlan didn't mean to shadow her as she made her way across the office, chatting with several people, asking questions of some, dealing with problems for others, but he was interested in seeing her work. She was efficient, friendly, and clearly well-liked.

She turned the corner into the bank of cubicles where he was hiding and spotted him.

He attempted to cover up for his stalking. "There you are. I was looking for you."

"Do you need something?"

Lochlan held up the file in his hand. "I was going to ask you to deliver this to Ron's office, but since I'm almost there, I'll drop it off myself."

"Okay. I was taking care of a few things out here. I'm about to head back to my desk."

"I've got a couple of items to discuss with Ron. I'll try to make it quick, so we can head out to your place."

She glanced around, clearly uncomfortable with his

comment. No one was around, but it was obvious she didn't want to discuss her personal affairs in the common area where they could be overheard. "Fine," she said softly, then continued to make her way back to the office, stopping to answer a question about sick leave.

His chat with Ron took longer than he'd intended, so he cut it short, intent on grabbing May so they could meet Sean.

"It's two forty-five," he said as he entered the office.

May looked up in surprise as Lochlan approached her desk. "Actually, I took care of things so we don't have to be there. My mother is at the apartment. I told her your uncle was coming. There's no need for either of us to leave work. He can take a look around and email me an estimate."

She made a good point, but Lochlan had wanted to pull Sean aside to covertly ask him about making repairs to more than just the kitchen. Her apartment was in bad shape. He'd noticed a cracked window, warped flooring in the living room and several places where the drywall was crumbling. He was also sure that the hallway and small dining area outside the kitchen were going to need a fresh coat of paint as well, thanks to smoke damage.

And all of that was just in the places he'd seen. He hadn't gotten a glimpse of the bedrooms or bathroom.

May had mentioned trying to save up to get a better place, and he knew she wouldn't accept his help in moving sooner, despite the fact his future brother-in-law, Lucas Whiting, owned more properties than Hilton had hotels. Which meant he'd like to at least make her current apartment livable.

He'd place a call to Sean later. "I'll concede the trip to your place on one condition."

"What's that?"

"You drop that Mr. Wallace crap once and for all."

"Fine."

He chuckled. "Just like that?"

"Would you have ever given up on the request?"

He shook his head.

"Then, yeah, just like that." She smiled and turned back to her computer. "Now, if you don't mind, *Lochlan*, I have work to do."

Lochlan had expected her capitulation to please him. Instead, the response was something stronger, less controllable.

He sucked in a deep breath and returned to his office. He needed to put some distance between them before he did something rash and irresponsible. He had told himself he was helping her because she was a good employee in need.

He was lying to himself.

Lochlan texted Sean to tell him May's mother would be there to meet him, then tried to read through the financial report his accountant had dropped off earlier, but he found it impossible to concentrate.

May had been with him just over two months. Two months, and already he was feeling the overwhelming desire to toss out every rule he'd ever lived by.

But he couldn't. She needed her job, needed the salary and —unbeknownst to her at the moment—the health insurance plan he was setting up to include her nieces and her mother.

A short time later, his cell phone rang, and he glanced at the number. He grinned when he saw Sean's name. Lochlan spun his chair toward the windows and lowered his voice.

"Hey, man. Good to hear from you. So what's the damage?"

"Lochlan, I'm at the hospital."

"What? Why?"

"When I got to May's place, no one answered. The door was unlocked, so I was concerned. There's no security system in the building. I found her mom in the bathroom, on the floor, in a lot of pain."

Lochlan stood up and turned back toward May's desk. She wasn't there. She must've gone to the ladies' room or out to one of the other offices to pick up some paperwork.

"Did you call an ambulance?"

"No. She wouldn't let me. Said it was too expensive. She didn't even want to go to the hospital, but I convinced her. Carried her down three flights of stairs and drove her here. ER doctor just took her back."

"Are you at Hopkins?"

"Yeah."

"May and I will meet you there. Thanks for everything, Sean."

"Meet him where?" May asked, walking into the office with a stack of folders.

"The hospital. It's Linda."

"Oh my God!" May spun around, racing toward her desk drawer to retrieve her purse. "What happened?" she called out as she did so.

"I don't know," Lochlan said as they walked to the elevator together. He texted as he spoke, asking the valet to bring his car to the front. "Said she was on the bathroom floor in a lot of pain."

He spotted the briefest moment of panic on her face before she willed it away, sucked it down. Lochlan got the impression May was a master of suppressing her emotions, but those things weren't going to stay buried forever. Somewhere down the road, she was likely to explode.

"It's going to be fine," May muttered. Lochlan noticed she

did that when she was stressed out, gave herself these little reassuring speeches.

He grasped her hand and squeezed it. "It *is* going to be fine."

She tugged her hand away from his, even though they were alone. "I'm so sorry. I'm making us leave work again."

He frowned at her apology. The elevator opened on the garage level and, mercifully, the valet was just pulling up with his car. May raced to the passenger's side, climbing in before he could reach for the door to open it for her.

Lochlan hopped in and put the Audi in gear, heading toward the hospital. He prayed they didn't hit a lot of traffic.

May glanced at the time. "The girls." She reached for her phone, then paused as if thinking.

"What time do they get out of school?"

May seemed to be struggling. "They're probably just now getting on the bus. Takes them half an hour to get home. No one's there. I need...um...shit..."

"Hang on." Lochlan dialed his cell. "Hey, Yvonne. Can you do me a huge favor? The two little girls who were with me at the restaurant the other night are on the bus heading home from school. Sean is with May's mom at the hospital, and no one is there to get them. They've met you before, so I was hoping you could pick them up and take them back to the pub for a little while. Maybe you can park them in front of the TV up in the dorm with whoever's home. Just until we see what's up with May's mother."

He smiled when he heard Yvonne's keys rattle.

"What's the address?" Yvonne asked.

He gave it to her. Then Yvonne promised to break every traffic law to get there before them. "Thanks, Vonnie. I owe you one." He disconnected the call. "She's on her way. You think the girls will be okay with her?" he asked.

May nodded. "Yeah. Chloe asked just this morning if we could eat Irish again tonight."

"Then she's getting her wish."

"You said she could park them in the dorm?"

"Silly name my family has for the apartment some of my cousins share above the pub. It's where my mom grew up with her parents and siblings. Always two or three Collinses kicking around up there. They'll keep the girls safe and sound until we get back."

May fell silent, her hands clenched in her lap. He watched her close her eyes, taking deliberate, deep breaths. The night of the fire, he'd admired her ability to pull herself together, to remain calm.

Today, for some reason, it was pissing him off.

They traveled the rest of the way in silence. Lochlan found a parking spot close to the ER entrance, and he grabbed her hand as the two of them walked into the waiting room. He spotted Sean instantly. His uncle was hard to miss. Like Lochlan, Sean was blessed with the same large frame as most of the other men in their family. They were a bunch of big, burly dudes, according to Riley.

"Sean," Lochlan said, guiding May toward his uncle. "This is May. May, this is my uncle Sean."

They shook hands.

"Thank you so much for bringing her here. Do you know where she is?"

"They pushed her back to an examining room about twenty minutes ago. I haven't seen or talked to anyone since. Oh wait," Sean pointed to a door opening, "that's the doctor."

The doctor approached them, looking at her. "Are you Linda Flowers's daughter?"

May nodded. "Is she okay?"

"She had a gallbladder attack. A rather nasty one, I'm afraid. Does she have a history of gallstones?"

May nodded. "Yes. She had a pretty nasty attack the year my father passed away. They discussed removing it, but because it was only her first time suffering from gallstones and she'd been under stress due to dad's passing, the doctor just prescribed medicine."

"I'm going to recommend that we take the gallbladder out. The procedure is called a cholecystectomy and it's a pretty noninvasive surgery. We'd like to keep her overnight and perform the procedure first thing in the morning."

"Wow. That's fast."

Lochlan didn't like how pale May had gone. He put his arm around her shoulders, tucking her close on the off chance she passed out.

She jerked at his touch, clearly not expecting it. She looked up at him and, once again, he noticed her struggling to pull herself together.

"May," he murmured.

"It's fine. I'm okay." Her voice belied a strength he simply didn't see in her face.

The doctor gestured toward a woman sitting in a nearby office. "There's some paperwork we need filled out, and we'll need your insurance information. Ms. Hartman can help you with that, and then I'll take you back so you can see your mother. She was asking for you."

May gave him a forced smile that didn't reach her pretty blue eyes. "I'll try to make this quick, Lochlan. I—"

He cupped her face in his palms and tried to give her a comforting smile. "Take all the time you need. I'm not going anywhere."

The two of them held each other's gazes for just a

moment, and then she walked to the business office, sitting across from Ms. Hartman.

"May is your new PA, right? The one who took Sally's place?" Sean asked.

Lochlan nodded. "Yeah."

"She's the one with the niece who stopped talking?" Sean was married to Lauren. Obviously, she'd told Sean about his call asking for help for Jenny.

"May's brother and his wife were killed in a car accident. May and her mother took in the girls. May gave up her bedroom to them. She sleeps on the couch."

"Wow. She seems pretty young to take all that on."

Lochlan couldn't argue that. "She is. She's amazing though. She stepped into Sally's shoes at work and never missed a beat. It's like she's always been there."

"I have to admit, I would have expected you to hire someone older after Sally."

"Sally hired her."

Sean grinned. "Then that makes sense. Damn if I don't love that woman even more now."

Lochlan frowned. "What are you talking about?"

"Seems to me Sally's parting gift to you was a potential girlfriend."

Lochlan snorted. "No. Sally was perfectly aware of my feelings regarding long-term relationships."

"She was aware of them, but did she *agree* with them?"

Sean's reply took Lochlan aback. There's no way in hell his former administrative assistant would have taken such a risk, would have played with Lochlan's business and May's feelings that way.

Of course, the woman *had* told him on more than one occasion she wouldn't let him make the same mistake she had, remaining married to her job rather than seeking out the real thing. But that was just talk. Or...

He was pretty sure that was just talk.

Lochlan had tried to call Sally a few weeks ago to see how her cruise to Mexico had gone. The voice mail message told him she'd booked another cruise, a longer one around the Mediterranean, and that she'd be out of reach for four more weeks.

Clearly he'd paid her too damn much. The woman was living it up in retirement.

He was also starting to suspect she was avoiding his calls on purpose.

When Lochlan walked over and sat down in the waiting room, Sean dropped down next to him.

"You don't have to hang around, Sean. We could be a while."

"Okay. I think I might head back over to May's apartment. The door was unlocked when I got there, and I was so worried about getting her mom help that I didn't have time to look for a key to lock up. I'll go back now and do the estimate on the repairs. The damage was pretty substantial."

"Can you take a look at the rest of the apartment as well? See what else needs to be done to make it safe for May and the girls. I only had a quick glance the other night, but I spotted some issues."

Sean nodded. "Yeah. So did I. I'm not crazy about the fact there's no security in the building."

Lochlan sighed. "I know."

"That's not a part of the city where you want to live without a secured entrance."

"You're preaching to the choir. Truth of the matter is, I only just learned where she lived a few nights ago. She also walks to and from work, can't afford a car."

"That's not good. Don't you put in some pretty late nights?"

Lochlan nodded. From now on, he would drive May home on those nights. "Yeah. I'm afraid I had blinders on in regards to her personal life. It's a lame excuse, but she's only been with me a couple of months and she's damn good at putting on a happy face, even when things suck."

"Only a couple of months, huh?" Sean was grinning widely at him.

"What's that look for?"

"The Collins curse took you down fast."

Lochlan shook his head. "Don't start. It's not like that. She's my assistant and she's going through a rough patch. I'm trying to help out. That's all."

"Mmmhmm," Sean hummed. "I'll send May an estimate in the morning."

"No. Send it to me."

Sean laughed as he stood. "You got it."

"It's not the curse," Lochlan said as his uncle walked away, laughing even harder.

Lochlan pulled out his phone and texted Yvonne. She'd arrived at the apartment building just as the girls were getting off the bus. They were grabbing a plate of cheese fries at the pub—Yvonne's idea of a healthy after-school snack—then heading up to the dorm. He promised her they'd get there as soon as they could, but Yvonne assured him there was no need to rush. Apparently, Chloe and Pop Pop had started talking about contemporary recess games, and he was giving her a rundown of how to play Red Rover.

Lochlan chuckled as he tucked his cell back in his jacket pocket. May had finished up in the office and gone back to see her mom. He chewed over Sean's concerns about the lack of security in May's building and came to a decision regarding tonight. One she wasn't going to agree to easily.

May had only been with her mother for half an hour when she returned to the waiting room.

"That was quick." Lochlan stood up. "Everything okay?"

"Yeah. They'd given her something for the pain and it was making her sleepy. Apparently, she's been dealing with the gallstones for a few days but didn't want to worry me. I'm starting to think her distraction in the kitchen was a result of how badly she was hurting."

Lochlan took her hand again as they headed for the exit. He got a sense of her wanting to tug it back, so he tightened his grip.

"How long will she be in the hospital?" he asked as they got into the car.

"It depends on how the procedure goes. If all goes well, she could be home by tomorrow night. If not, it'll be a few days and a longer recovery."

Lochlan pulled out of the hospital parking lot, wondering how long it would take before May realized he was heading in the wrong direction. It spoke to her level of distraction that he was nearly back to her apartment before she remembered the girls.

"Wait!" she called out. "We have to go to the pub for Chloe and Jenny."

"We are. We're hitting your place first."

"Why?"

"So that you can pack an overnight bag for you and the girls. You're all staying at my place tonight."

May shook her head adamantly. "No."

Lochlan parallel parked on the street outside her building and turned the car off. Twisting to face her, he laid out all the reasons why he wasn't taking no for an answer. "I don't want you and the girls spending another night in that smoky apartment. There's no security on the front door, and to be honest, your neighborhood sucks."

"None of that is going to change by tomorrow, so I'm not sure what difference one night will make."

May had a point, but he wasn't in the mood to be reasonable. She was walking a razor's edge, barely keeping it together, and he didn't want her to be alone tonight. Didn't want her to have to paint on a happy face for the girls. He was going to help her put them to bed in one of his guest rooms, and then he was going to offer her a shoulder to cry on.

May needed a good cry. It looked like she was long overdue.

"It's just one night, May. I have a big condo—three bedrooms and they all have their own bathrooms. Plenty of room for you and the girls."

"This is completely inappropriate. Lochlan, you have to understand that. You're my *boss*, and I can't..."

"Can't what?"

She opened her mouth, but nothing came out.

"I'm not inviting you to *my* bed. I'm simply offering you *a* bed."

"I didn't mean—"

"I know you didn't, but I think it needs to be clarified anyway. You've got dark circles under your eyes, and I can tell you're not sleeping well on that couch. You're working overtime to keep your family afloat, and I respect that. But you don't have to do everything alone, May. There's no shame in asking people for help."

She leaned back in the car seat, her gaze fixed straight ahead. "I need to do this on my own."

"Why?"

"We aren't your responsibility. This isn't your problem to

fix. It's mine. I can't start leaning on you because it wouldn't be fair to you. You barely know me."

"I don't think you have to know someone a long time to take their measure. I'm actually a very good judge of character."

She started to shake her head.

"Turn it around the other way. You've only known *me* a couple of months as well. Do you think you know me?"

May faced him. Time to lay the cards on the table. It was the only way. "Yeah. I think I have a pretty good idea of who you are. You're a nice man from a wonderful family. You're a cutthroat businessman. All of that is fine. It's the other part that's problematic."

"What other part?"

"You are a born protector, Lochlan. You would have been a knight in the Middle Ages. You were a normal, demanding boss right up until you walked into my crappy apartment the other night. Then, boom. The chain mail went on and now you're stepping in to save the day. I'm not a damsel in distress. I know my life is pretty shitty right now, but you know what? It's *my* life. *My* shit. I'll deal with it."

Lochlan grinned. "You've got it wrong."

She shook her head. She'd nailed it and she knew it.

"I'm a warrior. I wouldn't have been a knight all those centuries ago. I would have been a Viking. And Vikings conquer."

"So you're trying to conquer me?" She meant the words as

a joke, but she realized once they were out, they had a completely different meaning.

"I think I might be."

"I don't understand."

"May, in the last six months, you've dealt with at least half a dozen big things that would have reduced most people to a fetal position in the corner for a few years or so. You don't cry. You don't rage or shake your fist at the world. You just keep pushing it all down."

"That's how I deal with things. I can't fall apart. I have too many people depending on me. I mean, what happens if I let all of that go, and then I can't pull it together again?"

"And that's the part I'm feeling the need to conquer. I wish I could explain why, but I can't. Which means you're going upstairs and packing those overnight bags."

She breathed out an annoyed laugh. "You're going to have to let me win some of these arguments."

He got out of the car, walked around and met her on the curb. Lochlan grabbed her hand, and this time, she let him. "I never *let* anyone win, but that's not to say I can't be beaten."

"That's good information to have."

They passed Sean on the stairs. "Hey, I was just about to text you. Found a key to the front door. I was going to drop it off at the pub, but since you're here..." Sean dropped the loose key in May's hand. "I'll work up an estimate on the kitchen and send it to you in a couple of days."

"Thanks for everything, Sean," May said.

Lochlan hung out in the living room as May went back to the girls' bedroom to gather up pajamas, toothbrushes and clothing for school the next day. She tried to grab everything she could quickly, her mind still whirling over potential arguments against doing this. Something other than "it's a mistake."

Nothing came to her. Probably because the place still smelled of smoke and she was relieved not to have to spend the night there. Her eyes were itchy and her throat sore from sleeping in the living room. At least the girls and her mom had fared better, having the benefit of doors they could close.

She returned to the living room to find Lochlan standing in front of an old picture hanging on the wall.

"Your family?" he asked.

May nodded, swallowing heavily. Not a day went by where she didn't miss her dad and her brother, Jeff, both of them taken away far too young. She knew her mother had been deeply affected by their deaths, her mind no longer as steady as it once was. Mom was easily distracted these days.

May's grief was compounded by the fact she felt as though she was failing with Jeff's little girls. They'd been ripped away from a lovely little house in a small town in West Virginia, away from their friends, and dropped down in this shithole in the middle of Baltimore with her.

No wonder Jenny didn't speak anymore. There wasn't anything good to say.

Lochlan didn't ask anything else about the picture, and she was grateful. The last three days had officially kicked her ass. She was out of steam, hanging on by a thread.

"Ready to go?"

She nodded, allowing him to take her hand yet again as they locked up and descended the stairs. May considered pulling it away, but the past few months with him had taught her he wouldn't let go even if she tried.

Lochlan took what he wanted, but she really needed him to stop holding her hand. Every single touch, every kind word, every sexy look was doing things to her she couldn't let them do.

She was completely, ridiculously attracted to her boss.

And while he was simply offering help and kindness at a time when she needed it, it was translating to something much different to her heart. It was compounding her feelings for him, taking her from mere crush to genuine infatuation.

They rode to the pub in silence. Exhaustion and stress were pressing down on her, making it hard for her to think about much of anything.

When they arrived, Lochlan took her in through the pub side this time. She'd caught a glimpse of the bar through the large open connection between it and the restaurant the night of the fire, but she hadn't really looked. The place was great, so warm and welcoming. Though it was only a Thursday night, there were quite a few people there, drinking and talking quietly.

A handsome bartender was chatting with an older gentleman as the two of them watched baseball on the large-screen TV hanging behind the counter.

"The girls are upstairs in the apartment. We can head there in a second. Right now, I'd like to introduce you to some people."

"More family?" she asked with a grin.

He chuckled at her joke, adding to it. "I'm pretty sure there are a few people in Baltimore I'm not related to. I just haven't met them yet." Lochlan guided her to the two men she'd just been looking at. "Pop Pop. Padraig. I'd like you to meet May."

"Ah," Lochlan's grandfather said as he turned toward them. May liked him the second she saw his sweet smile and twinkling eyes. "The new assistant. I was wondering when you were going to make it into the pub."

"It's nice to meet you, Mr...." she paused, realizing she didn't know his last name.

"The last name is Collins, but you're going to call me Pat."

May laughed lightly. "I'm starting to see where Lochlan gets his demanding nature."

Padraig lifted the empty glass he was washing in a mock cheers. "She's already got your number, I see."

"Those two pretty little girls currently watching SpongeBob upstairs wouldn't happen to belong to you, would they?"

May nodded. "My nieces. I hope they weren't too much trouble."

"*Och.*" Pat waved off her concerns with a knobby hand that had her wondering how old he was. "'Twas nice to have some kids around here again. My grandchildren seem to be in no hurry to give me any great-grandkids."

"Take it easy there, Pop Pop," Padraig warned. "You know the K word causes Lochlan to break out in hives."

"K word?" May asked.

Lochlan didn't seem to want to reply, but he didn't have to.

Padraig was happy to explain. "Kids. Lochlan has sworn off the institution of marriage and fatherhood forever."

May wished that information didn't bother her so much. It wasn't like she could act on her feelings for Lochlan. That would be the height of stupidity. However, that didn't mean she thought he'd made a smart decision. "That's a shame," she said to Lochlan. "I think you'd be a great dad."

"I'm a workaholic," he muttered. "You know that."

"Yes, but you don't have to be," she murmured back. "You have very capable employees working for you who are able to shoulder more responsibilities if you wanted to get out and have a social life, maybe settle down and start a family."

May had no idea where this argument was coming from. It certainly wasn't her battle to wage. She didn't have a horse in the race.

"Sally chose well," Patrick said, watching them with great interest.

Lochlan rolled his eyes. "Don't you have a baseball game to watch?"

"This is more interesting," the older man teased.

"Come on, May." Lochlan tugged her closer, his arm around her shoulders. "We need to go get the girls before Yvonne corrupts them forever."

Padraig poured a pint from one of the taps for a man who walked in who looked exactly like him. "Pretty sure you're too late to save them. Colm," he said with a jerk of the head toward her. "That's May."

She lifted her hand to wave, expecting them to step back to talk to the man who was obviously Padraig's identical twin brother, but Lochlan continued tugging her away.

"No time to chat, Colm," Lochlan called out over his shoulder.

"A little competition is healthy, Lochlan," Colm replied.

"What was that about?" May asked as they entered a small stairwell at the rear of the bar.

"Nothing," Lochlan said. "Colm's a hopeless flirt. I thought I'd spare you."

May giggled. "I'm pretty sure I could handle it. Turns out *none* of the men in your family are hard to look at."

Lochlan narrowed his eyes good-naturedly, pretending to warn her as they walked upstairs. "He's a scoundrel. Steer clear."

"Not sure which sounds more dangerous. Scoundrel or Viking."

"Mr. Wallace!" They heard Chloe a split second before they saw her. The second they reached the top of the stairs, she was there, leaping into Lochlan's arms.

May was surprised—given Padraig's tidbit—that he was

prepared, lifting her and swinging her around as she squealed with delight.

Yvonne was sitting next to Jenny on the couch, French-braiding her niece's hair.

"Jenny," May said. "Look at your hair. It's beautiful."

Jenny didn't reply, but for the briefest of moments, May thought she saw a ghost of a smile. It brought tears to her eyes. She cleared her throat, swallowing it down.

Lochlan walked over to a beautiful brunette, giving her a quick kiss on the cheek. "Caitlyn, I didn't know you were here."

"Wedding planning," Caitlyn replied, though she was looking at May. "And you're the new PA. A few words of wisdom for you from someone who knows. Lochlan's bark is worse than his bite."

Lochlan rolled his eyes. "May, this is my sister, Caitlyn."

"She's getting married," Chloe said, wiggling to get out of Lochlan's arms so she could show May a picture in a magazine. "This is her dress!"

"Wow, it's lovely." There was no question Caitlyn would rock the dress. Or that it cost about a gazillion dollars. May had never seen anything so beautiful.

Chloe started flipping the pages. "And here are some flower girl dresses. Caitlyn's not having a flower girl, but I told her I'd do it."

May put her hand on Chloe's shoulder. "I'm sure she appreciated the offer, but you can't really invite yourself to be in someone's wedding, Chloe."

Caitlyn laughed. "Believe me, I'm tempted by the offer. She's adorable. The only thing holding me back is I'm pretty sure she'd steal the show."

"When's the wedding?" she asked.

"Two weeks from Saturday. I thought I had everything

well in hand up until a few days ago. Now I keep thinking I'll never be ready in time."

Yvonne shook her head. "You've planned the perfect wedding, Cait. Don't be crazy. Besides, Lucas would be just as happy to marry you down in the pub with you wearing nothing more than a feed sack. The man is ridiculously in love with you. That's all that matters."

May had never met such a kind, easygoing family. She genuinely liked every single one of Lochlan's relatives.

"I'm sure it will be everything you've ever dreamed of," May reassured her. "And, Yvonne," she said, "I can't thank you enough for this afternoon."

"It was no problem at all. These two cutie-pies are awesome company. We had a snack and went ahead and got the homework nightmare over with." Yvonne and Chloe shared horrified looks they'd clearly practiced.

Chloe dropped the magazine, reaching up and, within seconds, she was back in Lochlan's arms. "Is Nana in the hospital?" Her voice betrayed her fear, and May wanted to alleviate it. Chloe had lost too much in her short life.

Lochlan beat her to the punch. "She's just fine. Needs a little procedure to get rid of some stones in her belly. What is your aunt May feeding all of you?

Chloe enjoyed the joke, but clearly thought Lochlan was being serious. "She's not feeding us rocks!"

"You don't need to worry, Chloe. Your nana will be out of that bed and solving puzzles on *Wheel of Fortune* again before you know it."

Chloe giggled. "I'd like to buy a vowel."

Lochlan tickled her as a reward for her silly joke. "What do you say we grab a pizza, and then you three are having a sleepover at my house."

"Yay!" Chloe shouted, squirming to be let down so she

could grab her backpack. "A sleepover! But..." She pulled up short.

"But?" Lochlan prompted.

"Can we have Irish food again instead of pizza?"

Yvonne finished Jenny's hair. "I'm afraid they might think cheese fries with bacon is Irish now."

Lochlan rolled his eyes. "We'll grab takeout from downstairs."

"Sleepover, huh?" Caitlyn said to Lochlan, obviously trying to tease him. "You're letting kids into the inner sanctum?"

Lochlan tilted his head and shot her a look May assumed was a warning.

"My house still smells strongly of smoke after the fire. We probably shouldn't have stayed there the last few nights." May figured she owed Lochlan for making the offer of his guest rooms. It was clear his family was starting to get the wrong idea about them. Best to help him put those rumors to rest before they started.

"Mmmhmm," Caitlyn said. "Sure." The amused glance she shot Lochlan told May her attempt to help him had fallen short. "It was nice to meet you, May."

They said their goodbyes then walked down to Sunday's Side—the restaurant was apparently named for Lochlan's beloved grandmother—and ordered four dinner specials to go before heading out.

May had expected Lochlan's place to be nice, but the reality of it blew her away. He lived in an upscale condo on the waterfront that took up an entire floor of a renovated warehouse. It was very urban and sleek, masculine yet cozy at the same time.

Chloe's eyes widened when they walked in, and she hurried over to the large window that faced the harbor, plastering her hands and face to the glass. "Wow. Look at all the boats!"

Lochlan crouched beside her and pointed. "See the one with the blue flag on top? That's mine."

"You have a boat?" Chloe asked excitedly. "Can we go for a ride on it?"

"Chloe," May said, trying to wipe away the fingerprints Chloe had left on the window. "Mr. Wallace has done enough nice things for us. We're not asking for—"

Lochlan interrupted May, placing his hand over hers to stop her from wiping the glass. "Of course we can all go out one day, Chloe. Not tonight though. It's a school night, and it's getting late."

May was touched by his kindness to her nieces. She was also frustrated by it, because it only deepened her attraction to him. If he had just been a pretty face, she might have been able to resist him.

Who was she kidding?

The man was six feet five inches of pure masculinity. Muscular, broad-shouldered, with light brown hair and dark eyes. Everything about his appearance was striking, attractive. That was deadly enough to her libido, but throw in his sense of humor and how sweet he was to Chloe and Jenny, and forget about it. She was a goner.

The four of them opened their "Irish" cheeseburgers—which tasted just like American ones, despite Chloe's insistence they were different—and ate at his dining room table together. Once again, Chloe and Lochlan carried the conversation, the two of them quite funny as they talked about their favorite Disney movies.

May had a hard time making his family's comments about Lochlan not wanting a family stick. He was a natural with kids.

After dinner, Lochlan showed Jenny and Chloe which room they would be staying in. It was a lovely bedroom with a queen-size bed and its own bathroom. Chloe climbed up on the tall mattress, falling back dramatically, claiming it felt like she was on a cloud.

Lochlan was amused, until May murmured he might not find it funny tomorrow when he tried to send them home. "Chloe might be tough to get out, now that you've let her in," May teased.

Lochlan didn't laugh. Instead, he gave her a funny look she couldn't interpret. If she didn't know better, she'd think he wasn't as bothered by that idea as he should be.

The girls took turns in the bathroom, brushing their teeth and getting into their pajamas. Once they were settled in the bed together, May bent over and kissed them good night. "You sure you don't want me to read you a story?"

Chloe shook her head emphatically. "Mr. Wallace is going to do that," she insisted.

"Lochlan," he said.

Chloe's smile grew wider. "Lochlan."

Lochlan raised an eyebrow at May as if to say, "See how easy that was?"

She narrowed her eyes, feigning anger, then left the three of them alone. She wandered back out to the living room, looking at the twinkling lights from the boats on the water. The same exhausted feeling that never fully left settled over her, pressing in until it was hard to breathe.

May's mom didn't have insurance. She'd never worked a day in her life, and when Dad died, the health insurance ran out. This procedure was going to cost them a king's ransom. Between it and the fire, May was going to be stuck sleeping on that crappy couch until she was fifty, and Jenny...

God. Jenny needed to see a psychologist, but May simply

couldn't afford that. She wasn't sure what Lochlan's aunt Lauren would say, but May was certain Jenny's issues couldn't be solved in one visit, and there was no way she could impose on her for more than that.

Lochlan kept trying to help her, but she couldn't let him do that either. For one, her problems weren't his, and for another, her feelings...

She pushed it all down, shoved every lousy, helpless thought deeper into the well. May couldn't fix any of it right now, so it was time to do her usual. Focus on one day at a time. It was all she could handle.

She sucked in a deep breath, but not enough air hit her lungs. The damn things had seized up, tightened. Lochlan hadn't shown her where she'd be staying. She wished he had. May needed to crawl into bed, close her eyes and just fucking give in to the panic attack. It was coming no matter what.

She lifted one of her hands to touch the window, hoping it would cool her off. She suddenly felt too warm as she struggled to breathe. Her fingers trembled, so she lowered her arm.

"May."

She turned in surprise. She hadn't heard Lochlan come in. "I..."

"Are you okay?"

May nodded. "I'm fine."

Her words prompted a scowl she couldn't understand.

"Dammit," he muttered, reaching out to her. "You aren't *fine*. Come here."

He drew her into his arms, wrapping her up in the warmest embrace of her life. Regardless of that, May couldn't relax. She tried to pull away, but his grip was iron-clad, solid.

"Hold still." Lochlan's voice was strong and deep, and there was something in those depths that called to her, made her want so much. Too much.

The tension in her shoulders gradually loosened, and she tentatively raised her own hands, placing them around Lochlan's middle, locking them at his back.

He started to slowly sway, the rocking motion soothing, peaceful. The panic attack began to ease. They remained that way for several minutes, May's muscles relaxing, her brain shutting down. It was bliss.

"That's better. Good girl," he murmured. "Just let it all go, May."

He had a way of driving away all the dark thoughts that she couldn't quite understand. He'd simply say her name, touch her, and everything vanished.

Eventually, they shifted apart. May pulled back to look up as Lochlan glanced down. The position put their faces close, their lips mere inches apart.

She wanted him to kiss her.

No, she needed him to kiss her. And there was something in his eyes, something wild and unstrained that told her he wanted the same...and more.

Her hands slid to his waist, and she gripped his shirt tightly as she fought an internal battle over whether to pull him closer or push him away.

Lochlan reached up, one hand cupping her cheek, his intent crystal clear.

He *was* going to kiss her.

Boss.

He's your boss.

She pushed back and turned toward the window once more, forcing herself to look down at the water, so she couldn't see his face in the reflection. Couldn't see how he reacted to her rejection.

She also couldn't lose her job. It was the only thing keeping her family afloat. Granted, they were all clinging to one crappy life preserver, but it was better than nothing.

"Tell me what you want, May."

"Want?" she asked, puzzled, refusing to turn and face him.

"Yes. What you want."

"I want my mom to be okay. I want Jenny to talk."

"I'm not talking about your family. I'm talking about you. Take them out of the equation. What do *you* want?"

She knew he meant something far more personal, private. She recalled her wicked fantasies of him over the past few months. His fingers gripping her hair as he kissed her roughly, the way he would push her facedown over his desk and take her from behind. Or the way she would straddle his lap in his desk chair and ride him. She wanted him to tie her up in a real bed—not on her crummy couch—and take over. Take charge.

She'd spent every minute of every hour for the past five years making every single decision—from what to eat for dinner, to figuring out how they were going to pay the electric bill. She was exhausted, and she needed someone to hold the reins for just a little while. Someone to make her forget how scared and tired she was.

She pressed her forehead against the window and sighed. She couldn't tell him that. So she lied. "I don't want anything. I'm fine, Lochlan."

"That's it. I've had it."

May's head flew up in surprise at the outright anger in his voice, and then she was twisted around. She dragged her feet as he grasped her upper arm and pulled her down a short hallway on the opposite side of the living room from where the girls were staying. Lochlan opened a door to a lovely bedroom decorated in shades of blue, her favorite color.

He followed her in and then—God help her—he shut and locked the door.

"Is this your room?" she whispered.

"No. It's yours. Mine is across the hall. I have some things to say to you, and I don't want the girls to overhear."

"Okay." May looked around the room. There was a chair next to a small desk, but that was the only place to sit in the room with the exception of the bed. She should leave the chair for him, but that meant... Even this decision defeated her at the moment.

She was feeling light-headed and—

Lochlan placed his arm around her waist and led her to the bed. "Sit down before you fall down."

She didn't want him to think she was weak. "I'm fine," she repeated, trying to instill some semblance of strength into the words.

He snorted derisively. "Of course you are. You're always fine. Even when you aren't."

"What are you talking about?"

"We're not at work."

She raised her hands in a "no shit" way, but Lochlan didn't crack a smile. Instead, he continued explaining. "When we're not at work, I'm not your boss."

May scowled. "Of course you are. You're my boss no matter where we are."

"No. Not here. Not away from the office."

"Why are you saying that?" she asked.

"You can't keep doing this, May." Lochlan continued to answer her questions with responses that didn't fit, that didn't make sense.

"Doing what?"

"Lying about your feelings. You aren't *fine*. You're miles

away from that. Pretending otherwise doesn't change the truth."

"And falling apart every three seconds doesn't either. My family—"

"Needs you. I get that. But what about what *you* need?"

She looked at him, her mind going completely blank. In truth, she couldn't think of anything she needed other than the ability to take care of her mom, Chloe and Jenny.

What she wanted, of course, was another thing entirely, but she couldn't have that.

Lochlan shook his head. "You don't know what you need, do you?"

May sighed, her shoulders tight with anxiety, her head starting to ache. "I..." She slowly shook her head.

"You need a way to relieve the pressure, to get some of these bad thoughts out before you explode."

"I don't know how to do that." She rose from the bed. She needed to get out of here, grab the girls and go back to her shitty, smoky apartment and crappy couch. She needed to figure out where she was going to get the money for her mom's surgery and how to make Jenny talk again and—

Her lungs closed up.

No. What she *really* needed was air.

"I can't stay...we have to..." She walked toward the door. "I'm fine," she choked out.

Lochlan was next to her in an instant, his hand on her upper arm, turning her toward him as he pushed her against the door. "If you say the words *I'm fine* to me one more time, I'm going to turn you over my knee and spank your ass."

May was shocked into silence for a full thirty seconds before she could form a single word. "What?"

"You heard me. Tell me you're fine one more time, and you're going to find that skirt of yours wrapped around your waist, your panties on the floor, and your body draped over my lap. You got it?"

"Wow," she whispered.

That was probably the hottest fucking thing anyone had ever said to her in her life. More than that, it confirmed that she wasn't the only one suffering from a bad case of kinky fantasies. Lochlan wanted the same things.

Was that what had prompted her unexpected response to him? Was there something unspoken in the way he acted around her that made her want to check all her troubles at the door and disappear into him for a night...or twenty? Had his darker desires somehow kick-started these lustful dreams in her?

For the first time since dinner, his lips curled up into a grin. "Is that a good wow or are you contemplating calling 911?"

"Do I need to call 911?"

He shook his head. "I'd never hurt you, May. Never make you do anything you didn't want. You say no and it's no. No questions asked."

"I'm tired," she whispered.

Lochlan cupped her cheek once more. This time she turned her face toward the sweet touch, soaking it up. "I know you are, sweetheart."

One night.

She knew what she needed. Turned out it was the exact same thing she wanted.

"Lochlan?"

"Yeah?"

May took a deep breath and prayed she wasn't making the biggest mistake of her life.

"I'm fine."

❈ 6 ❈

Lochlan's entire body went tight as he tried to come to grips with the avalanche that had been slamming over him since seeing May's home, learning about her family, her life.

Never, not once in his thirty-one years, had he felt like this. Felt this overpowering need to take over.

Which was ridiculous when he considered it. After all, he was the CEO of a large company, a dominant lover by nature, a man used to being in charge. All of that came natural.

But that wasn't what he wanted here. This was something so much more primal, unstoppable.

He wanted May.

Wanted her body, her heart, her soul. Wanted the two little girls down the hall to stay there forever, wanted to make more kids with her, wanted to shoulder all her problems for her. He never wanted her to sleep on a couch again. Nothing but soft beds and feather pillows would be good enough for her.

Lochlan wanted everything he'd spent a lifetime avoiding.

Those feelings crashed in on him the second he saw Chloe wrapped around May's legs, saw the genuine love in her eyes, even as she took in the wreckage of her apartment.

Hell, he wasn't sure he didn't start to feel that way the first day she'd walked into his office, facing him down despite his rudeness, looking him straight in the eye and telling him she could do the job. More than that, she'd convinced him—right then and there—that she could. And she had.

This woman was invincible.

And she was going to be *his*.

He grasped her waist, pulling her lower body against his own, letting her feel exactly what impact she was having on him.

She didn't shy away, didn't demure or pretend that his hard-on wasn't there.

Lochlan started to lower his head, but she turned her face away, shaking her head. "You can't kiss me."

He placed a finger under her chin, forcing her to look at him. "Why not?"

"Because that would introduce an emotion to something that should probably just be physical."

"You're right," he said, not giving in. "It would."

"That wouldn't be smart."

Lochlan tilted his head as he looked at her. "Actually, I think it would be."

Before she could lodge any further complaints, he placed his lips on hers and kissed her, hard. Their lips parted at the same time, and he dipped his tongue inside her mouth, tasting her, breathing her in.

When May's arms wrapped around his neck, he deepened the kiss even more. He could spend the rest of the night doing nothing more than this, but that wasn't what May needed.

He gently broke the union.

And realized in that second, he was a true Collins...and the curse really *was* a blessing.

As he looked at her, he knew this was it for him. This was what he wanted his life to be. Him and her. And whatever else came with that. Families, work, health concerns, children, maybe a cat or two.

His hands drifted down to her skirt, and he slowly inched it up as the two of them studied each other's faces. May's face was flushed, her eyes heavy-lidded, her expression one of certainty. It was a welcome change from earlier at the hospital, when she'd looked frantic, terrified, worried.

Her skirt wasn't super tight, but it was snug enough that once the material was bunched around her waist, it stayed.

He ran his hands over the cheeks of her ass. She was wearing practical boy-cut panties, something that felt right for her. May wasn't the thong type. He pressed his fingers beneath the soft cotton, stroking the silky skin of her ass.

Her eyes drifted closed for a long moment, before opening to look at him once more. She wasn't shying away from this, from *him*.

Lochlan tugged her panties down, May helped by shifting her hips to ease the path. When they fell to the floor, she stepped out of them.

He kissed her again, unable to stop himself, to move them to the next level. If he could freeze time right here, with his lips on hers, he would do it.

May's fingers ran along his chest and he longed to strip off his own clothing, to feel her hands on his skin.

He wanted everything...right now. But more than that, he needed to know she was okay with this. Today's culture, its climate, had him feeling overly protective of her. He had to know this was truly what she wanted, that she wasn't feeling coerced or scared. "May. You can say no at any point and I'll stop."

She smiled at him. "I'm fine," she repeated, purposely using the words to taunt him, to get him to move on to the next part.

He grinned, even as he grasped her arm and pulled her to the bed. Lochlan sat down, then tugged her over his lap. May didn't resist. She wasn't going to pretend to fight him. When she looked over her shoulder at him and smiled, he couldn't resist for a second longer.

He lifted his hand and brought it down on her ass, roughly, with enough force to show her exactly what she had invited.

She jumped in surprise, but didn't try to push away. So he smacked her again. And again.

As he spanked her, he told her what to expect from now on. "I'm going to do this every time you lie to me, May. Every time you tell me you're fine when I know you aren't. You can't keep bottling things up, pretending you aren't hurting or scared."

May's legs parted slightly and he accepted the unspoken invitation, pressing two fingers inside her.

"God," she groaned. "Yes." She was dripping wet, her pussy clenching tightly. She was already at the precipice, close to going over.

"I'm going to help you forget, going to show you a better way to handle things. When you're overwhelmed or starting to panic, you find me. I'll make it all go away."

Lochlan withdrew his fingers despite her complaint and spanked her again. Her ass was pink, hot to the touch, yet she'd begun to anticipate his swing, rising up to meet them, asking for more.

A dozen strokes in, he heard it.

A soft cry.

Finally. She was letting go.

He tried to lift her, pull her up to comfort her, but she shook him off. "No. Keep going. More."

"May, you're crying."

"No I'm not," she lied, the thick sound of her voice betraying her.

"Let me hold you."

Her eyes were full of challenge when she looked up at him and spat out the words, "I'm *fine.*"

May wouldn't give in easily. She'd clearly spent too many years suppressing her emotions. Lochlan wanted her to be able to release that pain with him, to trust him enough to shoulder some of the load, but she wasn't there. Yet.

He spanked her again, then drove three fingers deep.

She reared up. "Oh my God! Please. Please, Lochlan."

He thrust in and out roughly. He'd intended to tease this out, make her wait, make her beg, but Lochlan changed his mind. May needed to come. Badly.

They had all the time in the world to learn how to draw this out. For now, he wanted to give her exactly what she needed.

She met his fingers on each inward push, shoving her hips back as much as she could in her position to add even more force. He knew the moment her body started to go over.

"May," a tiny voice called out from across the condo.

She stopped moving, going perfectly still.

Everything in her shut down in an instant. One second she was lying across his lap, the next she was standing several feet away, tugging her skirt down.

She was breathing heavily, her face red. He watched as she tried to shake off the residual effects of her denied orgasm, her trembling hands smoothing the wrinkles out of her skirt.

"May," Lochlan said, trying to help her calm down. "It's okay."

"I shouldn't have...I...we...that was a mistake."

He shook his head as he stood. He wasn't about to let her go there. Nothing about what they'd just done was wrong.

"No. May, listen—"

Chloe called out her name again. The little girl's voice was sleepy and uncertain. No doubt she'd woken up in a strange place and gotten scared.

"I have to go to her."

Before he could say another word, May had the door open and was gone. He walked to the doorway, watching as she rushed across the living room and disappeared into the other guest room. He took a few minutes to calm himself down, trying to will away the rock-hard erection.

May had to be hurting as well.

When he felt more composed, he walked toward the girls' room. He heard May reading from a book she'd packed in their overnight bag. Leaning against the hallway wall outside the door, he listened to the rhythmic pattern of the story about a grandmother and a sleeping child in a napping house.

He started to push away from the wall when the story ended, but Chloe's voice stopped him.

"I miss Mommy and Daddy."

Lochlan's throat tightened at the pain in the child's voice.

"I miss them too," May said.

Chloe sounded near tears when she said, "I want to go home."

"We'll go home first thing in the morning."

"No," Chloe said. "I mean *my* home." She started crying quietly as May made soothing noises.

Lochlan's heart broke for all of them. They'd lost so much at such young ages. And not just Jenny and Chloe, but May as well. Sometimes he had to remind himself she was only twenty-four years old. They'd celebrated her birthday like everyone else's in the company a month earlier. He'd given her a stupid gift card to a local restaurant.

"It's going to be okay, Chloe. I'm right here and I'm always going to take care of you. I know it's been a rough week, but we're going to be okay. We've got each other and we're going to be," Lochlan heard the slight hitch in May's voice when she said, "fine."

He walked back to the living room and poured himself a scotch, sipping it slowly as he stood by the window, in the same spot May had occupied earlier, and studied the lights on the water.

After an hour had passed, he walked back to the guest room and peered inside. May was nestled in the middle of the bed, both girls curled against her, the three of them sound asleep.

For thirty-one years, he'd plowed headfirst through his life, working hard to build a thriving business while eschewing romantic relationships, believing success and financial security were the end goal.

He was wrong. The end goal was *this*. A woman to love. A family to provide and care for. A home that would keep all of them safe.

Lochlan went to his own bedroom and dropped down on the bed. Then, he reached for his phone and dialed.

"Hey, man. You're calling late. I was just about to turn in."

Lochlan knew Padraig would still be awake. He closed the pub at eleven, then walked to the apartment he'd shared with the love of his life, Mia, before her untimely death.

"When did you know, Paddy?"

"Know what?"

"Know that Mia was the one for you? That you loved her and wanted to be with her no matter what?"

"The night she came into the pub, fighting back tears after talking to the doctor. I followed her out and she told me about the brain tumor. She was the bravest, strongest person I'd ever met, and I just...knew."

Lochlan sighed. Mia had died six months earlier, she and Padraig stealing not quite a year together before the tumor took her life.

"You figured it out, didn't you?" Padraig asked.

"Figured what out?"

"May Flowers."

Lochlan chuckled. "No one likes a know-it-all, Paddy."

His cousin laughed, unoffended. "There was something about the way you described May at the pub that first night, the way your back went up when Finn and Colm joked about asking her out. It reminded me of the way I'd felt about Mia after spending that whole night walking around and talking to her. It's like there was suddenly a light inside me that had been turned off my whole life. Then I met her and it flashed on, lit up everything inside, and all of a sudden, I wasn't looking at my world in shadows. I could see it all clear as day."

Every word Padraig said rang true. Lochlan had thought his life was settled. Now he realized he'd just been waiting for *her*. He cleared his throat and searched for something to say that wouldn't give away how much his cousin's words had affected him. "I swear you're getting more like Pop Pop every damn day."

"That might be the nicest thing you've ever said to me."

Lochlan laughed. "I mean it, Paddy. I needed to hear all of that. It helped."

"You know Pop Pop fell head over heels for Grandma Sunday the first night he saw her. He told me the story once."

"Must be something to do with the name Patrick," Lochlan joked, considering his never-used first name.

"Or the Collins curse. Falling fast and hard doesn't seem restricted to just us Pats."

"Problem is, May isn't there yet. She's got a lot on her shoulders and I don't think she's going to be able to let her guard down."

"Plus you've only known her a couple of months. Declaring your undying love after that short amount of time will probably make you come off as slightly insane."

Lochlan knew that. "I haven't said anything to her yet. And I'm not going to. I'm only letting *you* know I'm insane. May will have to figure that out later."

"Sounds like a smart way to play it."

Then Lochlan groaned, something else occurring to him. "You're going to tell Colm about this conversation, aren't you?"

"Calling him the second we hang up. After all, he predicted you'd be the next to go down."

"You know, I'm living for the day love bites him in the ass too."

"You and me both, cuz. And, um, I just want to make sure you realize..." Padraig obviously wasn't comfortable with whatever he wanted to say next.

"Realize what?"

"You know May comes with an instant family. Two of the K words."

"That's not a problem. Not at all." It wasn't. Because it wasn't just May who'd slipped into his heart. The protector in him wanted to make everything better for those two sweet, broken little girls. They deserved a hell of a lot better than the shit life had given them so far. Luckily, he had the time and money to spoil them properly.

"Wow," Padraig said with a chuckle. "Major fall. Bet that hurt a little. You good?"

"Yeah. I've got a bit of work to do, but I know what my end goal is, and I'm not giving up until I get there. I can't."

"Welcome to the blessed Collins club. It's about time you succumbed to the so-called curse. Night."

"Good night."

Lochlan disconnected the call and tried to figure out his next move. He realized he was at least seventy-two miles ahead of where he should be, but he'd never been the type to move slowly. He decided what he wanted and then he worked tirelessly to get there.

He walked to the bathroom, taking a quick shower. It was nearly midnight, but he was wide awake, wired.

When he returned to the room, he saw he had one missed text. A group one from Colm telling Finn he owed him twenty bucks.

Great. By tomorrow, his whole family would know he'd fallen for his admin assistant. Funny how that didn't bother Lochlan a bit.

He laid down in bed, sleep taking him quicker than he expected.

Lochlan was almost surprised when he woke the next morning. The sun was shining through the window, and a glance at the clock told him he'd forgotten to set his alarm.

He hopped out of bed, tossed some lounge pants on over his boxers and walked through the living room to wake May and the girls. At this rate, Chloe and Jenny would be late for school, and he and May late to work. Good thing he was the boss.

The guest bedroom was empty, the bed made, everything put back so perfectly, he might not have known anyone had even slept there.

Walking back to the living room, he saw a note on the table near the door.

Lochlan,

Took a cab back to our place so I could get the girls on the bus to school. Mom's surgery is at nine. I might be a few minutes late to work, but I will make up the time, I promise.

Thank you so much for all your help last night.

May

Lochlan frowned. The only thing positive in the note was the fact that she'd called him by his first name and hadn't tried to revert back to that Mr. Wallace crap.

"One step forward, thirty-seven back," he muttered to himself.

Lochlan returned to his room to get ready then headed to work. More than a few employees glanced up in surprise to see him coming in an hour late.

He'd only been there half an hour, which had been just enough time to fix a few things on his calendar, before May arrived. She rushed inside and came straight to his doorway.

"I'm here. I'll have your coffee ready in just a minute."

"May, wait."

She hesitated, clearly hoping to make a quick escape. "Yes?"

"What time did you leave my place this morning?"

May was surprised by the question. "I don't know. I guess it was around six."

That would explain the dark circles under her eyes. She was the picture of exhaustion at the moment.

"Did you really take a cab, or did you walk?"

She opened her mouth, but he stopped her before she could dig herself into a hole. "Don't lie," he warned.

May sighed, a sure sign she had intended to. "We walked."

"You realize it's got to be a good two miles from my place to yours. I would have driven you home."

She shrugged. "It's a pretty day. Besides, we're used to walking."

Lochlan was working hard to keep his temper in check, but she was testing all his limits. The woman made it impossible to help her. "Come in here."

She looked over her shoulder, but did as he asked. She was only two steps into the room when he stopped her. "Close the door. Lock it."

May shook her head. "We're at work now. You're the boss again."

"That's right. I am. Lock the door."

His words came out more gruffly than he'd intended, but he hadn't liked waking up to find her gone. Her absence, coupled with the way they'd left things unfinished last night, bothered him.

She locked the door, then leaned against it. If he weren't so annoyed, he might have laughed at the fact she thought staying on the other side of the room would change anything he planned to say.

"How's Linda?"

"They had to push the procedure back. She's going in late this afternoon and they'll most likely keep her another night."

He glanced at his calendar. "My afternoon is clear. Actually, my whole day is."

She frowned. "No. It's not. You have several meetings."

"I shifted things around, moved the meetings back. I'll head over to the hospital with you."

Lochlan waited for her to reject the offer. She didn't disappoint him. "That's not—"

"Necessary. I know. I'm doing it anyway."

He walked around his desk, but didn't cross the room. "You look tired."

"I fell asleep with the girls." She rubbed her neck. "Must've been at a funny angle. I woke up at three with a stiff neck."

"Is it okay?"

"It's nothing."

"I didn't hear you leave."

She shrugged. "Like I said, it was early. We tried to be quiet so we wouldn't wake you."

"Grab your things, May. We're taking the day off."

May didn't reply, which proved to him exactly how tired she was. He couldn't stand seeing her so quiet, so defeated. He cut the distance between them, reaching for her. Drawing her into his arms, he released the breath he didn't know he was holding when her arms circled his waist, returning his hug.

"I'm here, May. And I'm not going anywhere."

"I have to...stop...I can't let you in, Lochlan. I'm sorry, but the way things are now, with my mom and the girls, they need me to be strong."

"You *are* strong."

"I don't feel that way...when I'm with you. I feel like I'm losing control. I can't do that."

Her words were muffled, her cheek pressed to his chest.

"You've got it wrong, sweetheart. Relying on me doesn't make you weak. It means you don't have to deal with all the pain, all the fears alone. Lean on me. I can help you get through this."

"I don't know how to do that! And I shouldn't. I mean, I know it probably looks like it's just been a couple of bad days, but the truth is, this is my life. Pretty much around the clock. You're a nice man and I know you want to help, but the best thing you could do for me is to just let me handle it. Please."

"No."

For the first time since she'd entered the room, May showed some spunk. Her temper flashed. "Dammit! You're not going to win this argument because I'm *right*. I know what I need. I know what's best for me." She stepped away from him, walking halfway across the room before whirling around in a fit of pique. "You just have to believe me when I say I'm fine!"

Her words were out before she could rethink them.

The second they passed her lips, the moment she saw his face, she understood her mistake. He could see it in the way her guard went up and her hands rose in front of her.

"I mean—"

"I know what you mean." He was standing next to her in an instant, his hand on her back, turning her toward his desk. He propelled her forward.

"What are you—"

Her question was cut off when he pressed between her shoulder blades, bending her over his desk against the flat surface. He followed her down, his chest snug against her back so that he could whisper in her ear.

"I told you what would happen if you lied to me again. Do you remember?"

"Yes." Her response was more breath than sound.

"I'm going to spank you—and you're going to come. Then I'm taking you back to my condo, to *my* bed. To sleep. From the looks of those dark circles under your eyes, you need at least eight weeks' worth, but you're going to have to settle for a few hours."

"My mom's surgery is at four. I have to get the girls off the bus and go—"

Lochlan stood up and slapped her ass. She was in another skirt. He didn't bother to lift it for the first few spanks because he didn't want to take the time. She needed the distraction.

"Lochlan," she whispered.

He considered the sound of his name on her lips a welcome change to her grocery list of never-ending duties, so he decided it was a good time to raise her skirt and tug her panties down. Her anxiety was starting to fade.

"Open your legs, sweetheart."

She did as he asked without comment. Progress. Her natural submissiveness was starting to override her strong sense of responsibility. All Lochlan had to do was prove to her she could have both. An outlet for all the worries pressing down on her and someone to help her shoulder her burdens.

He ran his finger along her slit, loving the sexy squeak his touch provoked. His dick was erect, thick, and all he could think about was driving into her, pounding deep and hard.

Lochlan wouldn't give in to that need. Not here. Not now. The first time he took May was going to be in his bed, and he was going to make love to her. This time was just for her.

He knelt down and ran his tongue along the same path he'd just stroked with his finger.

May jerked and tried to close her legs. "Lochlan!"

He gripped her thighs, holding them apart, as he pressed his tongue inside her, loving the little sounds escaping from her lips. May didn't hold back her enjoyment. After a few minutes, he stood again, slapping her ass half a dozen times more, until her hands were balled up in fists she beat against the surface of his desk.

"Please. Lochlan. God. I need...something more."

He shoved two fingers deep, fucking her tight hole roughly with them as she met him blow for glorious blow. Her back arched as she came, but very little sound emerged. It was as if she didn't have the breath for sound, but the way her body trembled told him exactly how intense the orgasm was.

She went limp as it waned, lying still, draped over his desk. Lochlan had never seen anything more beautiful. A small niggling voice in the back of his head had him questioning her experience, but he ignored it. There would be plenty of time for them to learn about each other's past relationships later.

He gave her a moment to compose herself before he helped her stand once more. He knelt to pull her panties back up, then draw her skirt down again. May's hands rested on his shoulders as she tried to steady herself.

She looked at him, her expression fluctuating between looking at him like he hung the moon and frustration that she'd succumbed to him once more. May wasn't finished fighting this thing between them.

He didn't care. He had the rest of his life to wear her down, to convince her that he was worthy of her love and trust. He had to. He couldn't imagine a life without her.

"Stop looking at me like that," she said as he rose and smiled at her affectionately.

Apparently, she wasn't the only one without a poker face. "Like what?"

"Like..." She paused, and it was clear she didn't want to say what she thought.

"Tell me."

She shook her head. "I'm tired. Seeing things. Forget it."

"Come on, May. We're going home."

"To *your* home."

He didn't correct her. At some point, she would understand that his home was wherever she was.

Until then, he'd let her make the distinction.

❧   7   ❧

When May opened her eyes, it took her a moment to figure out where she was.

"Shit!" She jerked upright, her heart racing when she realized it was late. It was growing dim outside, the sun sitting too low to provide much light. Glancing around, she found a clock on the nightstand.

"Seven-thirty? Oh my God!" She scrambled from the bed, muttering to herself.

"Why would he let me sleep so late? The girls...Mom!" Panic ensued as she hastily threw on her skirt and blouse. She had shed both just before she'd climbed into Lochlan's bed earlier in the day. Actually, he'd taken them off her, then tucked her in with the sweetest kiss she'd ever received.

Nine hours ago.

May grabbed her shoes and darted out of his room, racing toward the front door.

She pulled up short at the sound of a little girl's giggle.

Following the sound, she stood in the doorway of the kitchen and tried to make sense of what she was seeing.

Lochlan was chopping salad fixings and tossing them in a bowl. Chloe was standing on a chair in front of the counter, stirring something, while Jenny was sitting at the table, decorating cookies with sprinkles. Her silent niece wasn't smiling exactly, but there was definitely an air of happiness about her.

"Did you forget to wake me up?"

Lochlan turned and smiled. "She lives," he said in a scary voice that prompted a giggle from Chloe. "I was just about to come get you. The girls and I almost have dinner ready."

"We made sgetti," Chloe chimed in.

"Spaghetti," May corrected. "I thought we were going to go to the hospital."

Lochlan walked over. "We were. But you were down for the count, so I called and spoke to your mom briefly on the phone just before her procedure. She said there was no point in coming over simply to sit and wait. Said we could do that just as easily here. I promised we'd all come by later tonight."

Chloe pointed to Jenny's creations. "We're taking Nana cookies to make her feel better."

May was fairly certain her mother wouldn't be allowed to eat them tonight, but she would like the gesture. "Those are beautiful, Jenny."

Her niece actually established eye contact with her, her typical scowl replaced with a more peaceful look. How had Lochlan done that? In just one night?

"Can I talk to you for a second?" May asked Lochlan.

He nodded, leaving instructions for Chloe to come get him when the timer for the garlic bread went off. "And stay away from the hot stove," he warned.

"Okay." Chloe hopped off the chair and started putting sprinkles on the cookies with Jenny.

As soon as they were out of earshot of the girls, Lochlan said, "Listen, May. I'm sure you're upset with me for—"

She cut him off with a kiss. She went up on tiptoe, reached for his face and pressed her lips against his.

If Lochlan was shocked by the impromptu affection, he recovered quickly. His hands found her hips, pulling her flush against him, and he teased her lips open, giving her a preview taste of dinner, a lovely blend of tomatoes and something sweet.

"Have you been sampling the cookies?" she asked when they parted.

He grinned. "Every good cook tastes the food before they serve it. Wise words from Aunt Riley. What was the kiss for?"

"I just wanted to."

Lochlan chuckled. "I can roll with that."

"I feel human for the first time in...forever."

"A few peaceful, uninterrupted hours of sleep can do that for you."

May considered that and realized he was right. Her current sleeping situation on the couch was less than ideal. For one thing, it was very uncomfortable. Add to that the long workdays and stress, and May couldn't recall the last night she'd managed to sleep more than three or four restless hours in a row.

"I didn't even dream. I'm not sure I rolled over."

Lochlan reached out, tugging the ponytail holder out of her hair.

"What are you doing?" she asked.

"I want to see your hair down."

She ran her fingers through it. "It probably looks a mess."

Lochlan lightly pushed her hands away, running his own fingers through her hair, and she recalled the way he had looked at her in his office this morning. At the time, she'd dismissed it, thinking she was misinterpreting it due to her exhaustion.

But he was doing it again. Looking at her like he cared about her, like she mattered to him.

Like he loved her.

No man had ever looked at her like that, so she didn't have a frame of reference. But she'd seen plenty of romantic movies.

She was wrong. She had to be.

"I need to get it cut, but I haven't had much time." Typically, she trimmed it herself, as well as the girls' and her mother's.

"It's beautiful. You should wear it down more often."

She lifted one shoulder casually, not bothering to explain why she wouldn't do that. She looked too young when her hair was down and if she was going to succeed at work, she needed to project a more mature persona.

Then something occurred to her. "How did the girls get here?"

"I was waiting for them at your apartment when they got off the bus. We packed bags for the three of you and came back here. I was surprised to find you still sound asleep, so we did homework and started dinner."

It was all too much. "I'll never be able to thank you enough for the past few days, Lochlan."

He smiled. "I don't need thanks. You're easy to be nice to."

"Lochlan," Chloe called. "The buzzer is going off!"

"Come on," he said, taking her hand. "Dinnertime. Then we'll head over to the hospital to check on your mom."

The next few hours flew by as they did just what Lochlan said. Thanks to the long nap, the delicious dinner, and the nice visit with her mother—who already looked a thousand times better—May felt stronger than she had in months when they returned to Lochlan's place.

They put the girls to bed together, each reading them a story, and then Lochlan poured them both a glass of red wine as they settled on the couch, enjoying the view of the water from his living room.

May took a sip of the wine and enjoyed the way it warmed her up from the inside out. She rarely drank—okay, she never drank—so she made a mental note to stop after this one or she'd be dancing on the table.

"How's your neck?" Lochlan asked.

She was confused by his question for a moment, then she recalled this morning. "Oh. It's okay. I just slept at a funny angle. Worked out the worst of the kinks on the walk home."

"What did your dad do for a living, May?"

May grinned as she recalled her father. "He worked for UPS, managed one of the offices, until he got sick."

"Sick?"

May swallowed heavily. "Lung cancer. Smoked when he was younger, but Mom made him quit after Jeff was born. He fought it for about two years."

"How old were you when he passed away?"

"Just shy of nineteen. I'd gotten the job as a receptionist at the tech firm and kept living at home to help pay bills and take care of Dad. My mom..."

"What's going on with her?"

Lochlan's words confirmed she wasn't the only one seeing it. Her mother's fading memory, her weak grasp on reality.

It also drove home the fact letting him in had shown him too much.

She didn't reply. Didn't know how. She hadn't even admitted what she suspected to herself, continually pushing the dark thoughts away. If she faced it, it would only reinforce how completely alone she really was.

Lochlan stretched his hand out, palm up. She slid hers into it.

"Dementia?" he asked.

She started to pull her hand back, but he clung tight.

"No," she insisted, unwilling to go there. "She's just under a lot of stress, and she's been grieving for years. It's taking her some time to bounce back, but she will."

Lochlan didn't push the point and she was grateful for that. She was grateful for a lot of things, actually.

"Lochlan, this week... Well," she said with a grin. "It should have sucked, but it didn't. You and your family have been so amazing. I wish there was some way I could pay all of you back for your kindness."

May was confused when her comment provoked a frown from him.

"When's the last time you asked someone for help?"

May took a sip of wine to stall, to give her time to think.

"You can't remember a time, can you?" he pressed.

She shook her head.

"Why don't you?"

May shrugged. "I don't know. I guess I don't like to bother people with my problems."

"What about girlfriends?"

"I lost contact with my high school friends after graduation." She'd actually begun pulling away from them before that. Her father had been ill, so she'd taken on a couple of part-time jobs her senior year and spent every free minute home with him, knowing their days were limited. It was crazy to think she looked back on so many of those days almost fondly, but that time with Dad was precious to her. They talked for hours about everything. It was as if he'd had a lifetime of wisdom, hopes, dreams and fears to impart to her, and she'd soaked it all up like a sponge.

"Other family?"

"My dad has a brother who's married with some kids, but they live in St. Louis. We haven't seen them in a few years."

"He wouldn't help out if you called?"

"I...yeah. He would. Okay," she said, blowing out a hard breath. "I get it. I have too much pride and not enough sense. I'll call Uncle Todd next week." The distance between her dad and her uncle had been physical, not emotional. He'd flown in to be with them the last few days before her father passed and taken charge of the funeral preparations. He had called once a week for months after Dad's death, but she'd always assured him they were fine. After a while, the calls dwindled to less often and he took her at her word in regards to how they were getting along, accepting the "we're fine" at face value. Her uncle wasn't rich, but he definitely would send them some money to help with the kitchen repairs if she asked.

Just the thought of asking made her uneasy.

"Put the wineglass down, May."

"Why?"

He narrowed his eyes, letting her know he wasn't going to repeat his request.

She did as he asked, placing the glass on a coaster. He did the same.

"There are two things we're going to have to work on."

"Work on?" she asked.

"You lie to me when you think it'll end a conversation quicker. You have no intention of calling your uncle, do you?"

She bit her lower lip, trying to figure out what was the smartest move. Tell the truth, continue the lie, or just pick up the phone and call Uncle Todd.

"Don't bother answering. That leads to the second thing we need to work on. Your inability to ask for help."

"You might have a better shot at getting me to stop lying," she joked.

"Very cute." He did look amused. She liked being able to make him laugh. It wasn't that he was a super serious guy. In truth, he had a great sense of humor, a quick wit. Maybe that was why she liked amusing him. Because it meant she'd said something genuinely funny.

"Ask me for something," Lochlan said.

"Like what?"

"Anything that would help you."

She wiggled her eyebrows provocatively, something she would never have done if not for the wine, the orgasm and the sleep. For the first time in ages, she actually felt energetic and frisky.

"*Not* sexual," he added.

"This lesson just got a lot less fun."

Lochlan laughed, but didn't back down. "Think about everything that's going on with Linda and the girls, and figure out the one thing that would help you the most, that would take away the most stress."

She leaned back, trying to play the game, but she wasn't sure how to reply. And not because the list wasn't as long as her arm, but because she would never ask anyone for any of it.

"Money?" he prompted.

May shook her head emphatically. "No. I pay my own way." Or at the very least, she carefully managed her ever-growing debt.

"Childcare?"

"That costs money."

"A new place to live?"

"Also money."

Lochlan sighed. "Let's start smaller. A night out. One

night away from your family to go out and do whatever you want, to have some fun."

That sounded like a dream, but also impossible. "I already spend too much time away. I need *more* time with them, not less."

"One afternoon off a week."

Suddenly this felt less like a friendly conversation and more like bargaining with her boss. She shook her head.

"May—" he started.

She had to appease him, so she picked something easy. "I'd like to sleep in a real bed. All night. One night. The couch is old and sunken in, which means there's this damn spring that hits me right in the middle of my back and drives me nuts."

It was a request, though she could tell he wasn't impressed. Regardless, he rose. "That's an easy thing to give."

He reached down for her hand, so she grasped his, the act almost instinctual after a few days of holding it. She expected him to lead her to the guest room, but Lochlan made no move to leave the living room.

Instead, he wrapped his arms around her waist and pulled her against him, his mouth coming down to cover hers in a deep, warm kiss.

May knew she should pull away, find a way to return them to the professional distance they'd maintained throughout the first few months of her employment. She also knew she wasn't going to do that.

Lochlan said she couldn't ask for what she wanted. He was right.

But that didn't mean she couldn't *take* what she wanted. And right now...that was him.

He broke the kiss, his eyes locked with hers.

"You're beautiful," he murmured.

She smiled, surprised by the sudden dampness of her

lashes. Was she paid so few compliments that hearing one made her cry?

May reached up and cupped his cheek, wanting very much to touch him, to keep this close connection between them alive.

Lochlan bent over, his intent confusing, until he put one arm beneath her knees and lifted.

She gasped as he carried her from the living room.

"I can walk."

He grinned, not bothering to look down at her, his eyes focused on his direction. "And I can carry you. We're both very skilled."

She giggled. "Smart-ass," she whispered, her taunt provoking a quiet laugh from him.

Lochlan walked straight to his bedroom once more. She had asked to sleep in a real bed and she had hoped it would be his.

However, she didn't assume it would be.

"There's another bed across the hall." She didn't want to sleep in it, but she felt the need to lay their cards out on the table in regards to exactly what was happening tonight.

"The only bed you'll *ever* sleep in when you're here is mine."

He placed her on her feet, then walked to a large, over-stuffed chair near the huge window and sat down.

May tilted her head curiously. "It's a big bed. You hardly have to sleep in a chair."

Lochlan smiled. "I have no intention of staying in this chair. You and I are going to share that bed."

A coy woman might have hidden the huge grin his comment produced, but May didn't have it in her to pretend. "Okay."

Lochlan leaned back, rubbing the lower part of his face

with his hand. She couldn't tell if he was thinking or hiding his own smile.

"I'm not your boss when we're here," he began.

"So you keep saying." She didn't believe those words now any more than she had earlier. There was no way to keep what they were *here* out of what they were at work. The sexually charged morning she spent draped over his desk proved that. This was going to bite them both in the ass if things went south.

He narrowed his eyes, clearly reading her thoughts. "However, I am still in charge."

Now it was her turn to scowl. "What do you mean?"

"Take off your clothes."

"What about yours?"

She recalled the way he'd made himself appear larger when they were confronting Jenks after the fire. Somehow Lochlan managed to repeat that feat now, even though he was still sitting in the chair. One moment, he was relaxed, friendly, the next, he appeared to be made of steel, pure muscle and might.

That trick performed for Jenks had made her feel safe and protected. Tonight, she felt like prey. And what was more alarming was the fact she wanted to bare her neck to the beast.

Lochlan was sitting casually, his legs crossed at the ankles, one elbow resting on the arm of the chair. It was his eyes that told her the truth, not his body.

One glance at them let her know he wouldn't ask again, nor would he be denied for long.

She was taking off her clothes. Period.

May slipped the button free on her skirt, then slid the zipper down. She shimmied the material over her hips, leaving her panties in place. Then she undid her blouse, adding it to the small pile of clothing on the floor. She remained before him in just her bra and panties for a moment, digging deep to find the courage to continue.

Lochlan's gaze was too intense, too powerful.

She wanted to run.

She wanted to give him everything.

He held his pose, but his body language continued to lie, to give the impression he was relaxed when she suspected he was anything but. Lochlan rubbed his lower lip with his index finger, considering her disrobing, not making any further comment. He reminded her of a live wire, one wrong move and she would be in for one hell of a jolt.

Right now, he wanted her naked, and he seemed to know that she was powerless to refuse, that she'd give him what he wanted. Whatever he wanted.

May wished she could understand this instinctual behavior of hers, this desire to do exactly as Lochlan commanded. She could control herself in all things, except this. In this domain, she was defenseless.

That idea should scare her, but in truth, being with Lochlan was the only place she felt free. Safe.

Reaching behind her back, she unclasped her bra. The straps fell loose and she shrugged the entire thing off. Bending slightly, she worked the panties off as well. Once she was completely naked, she did the hardest thing of all. She held her arms at her sides and let him look his fill as her eyes remained locked on his face.

"Come here, May."

She had taken three steps before she even finished processing the request. She closed the distance between them, not stopping until she was a few feet from his chair.

Lochlan reached for her, his hand idly stroking her hip for a few seconds, before he straightened. "Straddle my lap, facing me."

Once again, she moved without considering the next step.

So much of her day was spent figuring out how to get from point A to point Z without losing everything. Right here, right now, she only had to obey. Lochlan would do all the thinking.

The chair was large enough to accommodate his request, and she briefly wondered how many women had joined him on it. She shoved that thought away.

The past had no more place here than the future. If she was throwing caution to the wind, it would only work if she remained in the present.

She started to sink down, but Lochlan used his grip on her bare ass to draw her even closer to him, so that as she lowered, her pussy rested against his erection, the material of his pants still a barrier between them.

Lochlan took one of her breasts in his hand, squeezing it gently before rubbing the nipple between his index finger and thumb.

"Are you on the Pill?"

She shook her head.

"Make an appointment tomorrow with your doctor."

"Lochlan—" she started.

"Don't, May. Don't give me the reasons why this isn't going to continue. Because it is."

She felt the slightest twinge of panic at his pronouncement. It went against the silent bargaining she was doing with herself, allowing herself just one night to indulge these desires before returning to life as usual.

A wise woman would get up and leave now. Or at the very least, a woman with half a brain would argue the point, try to make the man see reason.

What she would *not* do was close her eyes and moan when

the man placed his lips around her tight nipple and sucked it hard.

She was officially an idiot.

May gripped Lochlan's hair in her fists, holding his mouth against her, her head thrown back as she tried to assimilate to the pure bliss of his mouth on her breast. He teased her sensitive nipple with his tongue and then—God help her—his teeth. Her pussy clenched, empty, needy.

She drew one hand down to the spot that needed stimulation, touching her clit, rubbing it as another, louder moan escaped.

That was as much as she was able to do before Lochlan's iron grip encapsulated her wrist, pulling her hand away. Lucky for her, she had two hands. Releasing his hair, she intended to resume stroking herself, but Lochlan caught that wrist as well, tugging both of them behind her back.

"Lock your fingers," he demanded.

She started to shake her head, the haze of pure need fading enough that she could see his frown. He looked...angry?

"Lock your fingers or I'll tie your hands behind your back."

That threat did nothing to soothe her. She suspected she was leaving a damp spot on the front of Lochlan's pants. She was too turned on, too wet.

He was still holding her wrists, so he knew the moment she complied, interlacing her fingers. His grip loosened.

"Hold them there until I say otherwise."

The new position thrust her breasts out farther, something Lochlan was ready to take advantage of. He resumed his sucking, his mouth taking one nipple then the other, back and forth, for too many torturous minutes.

May started to squirm, trying to press her clit against his

erection, seeking some much-needed stimulation. Lochlan put an end to that by gripping her hips, holding her in place.

She cursed, but that only provoked a warning glance from Lochlan. Common sense fled in the face of genuine painful need.

Her fingers unlocked. Moving quickly, she managed two quick strokes before her world went topsy-turvy. One minute she was straddling his lap, the next, Lochlan had her on her back in the center of his bed, tying her spread eagle to the four posts.

He made quick work of her arms because it took her that long to figure out what he was doing. She presented more of a challenge with her legs, fighting desperately to rub her thighs together, to calm the overwhelming ache that wouldn't go away until it was filled.

"Lochlan, dammit—"

He cut her off. "Think long and hard about your next words, May. Any other woman would have found herself over my lap, getting her ass spanked already."

She'd been on the receiving end of that particular "punishment" before. It felt too good to encourage correction.

"Let me clarify," Lochlan said. "I would use my belt...and you wouldn't enjoy it."

May stilled—and it occurred to her she'd let this go too far without words, without explanation. "I don't understand what we're doing here."

Lochlan was kneeling between her legs, one ankle in his hands. He'd intended to tie it to the bedpost. That was when May realized the straps holding her hands had already been there.

He dropped her foot, coming over her body, caging her beneath him. He remained fully dressed, something that hadn't felt weird until that second.

Lochlan kissed her softly, then cupped her face, looking into her eyes. "Bondage wasn't my intent tonight."

"What was?"

"Honestly? I simply wanted to make love to you, but you touched yourself and...things escalated, went in the wrong direction."

"Control issues much?" she teased.

He grinned. "Always. And we're going to talk about that. Later. Tonight is going to be about something else."

As he spoke, he unfastened the straps at her wrists. May was equally parts relieved and disappointed by her sudden freedom.

She lowered her arms and decided she wasn't relieved at all.

"You like being tied up, don't you?" he asked.

May nodded.

"We'll do it again, May. I promise."

"Why do you have straps on your bed?"

Lochlan kissed her, not in an attempt to stop her questions, but because it seemed as if he couldn't resist her lips. She felt the same way.

"Tomorrow," he murmured against her mouth. "I'm not sure I have the patience to explain it all tonight."

He pushed away from her, standing beside the bed. May started to sit up, but he stopped her with a simple shake of his head.

She resumed her position, her legs closing.

Lochlan reached for one ankle, tugging it toward him. "Keep your legs open. Put your hands next to your head, palms up."

She did as he asked, grinning as she assumed the position. "Feels a bit like a surrender."

Lochlan didn't pretend that wasn't his intent. "Exactly. I

know there's a part of you that's still resisting me, fighting this. But not tonight."

May might have tried to respond to that, but Lochlan had started to undress as he spoke, and her attention was distracted by his bare, broad shoulders, ripped abs, and then...

She gasped when his pants and boxer briefs hit the floor.

"Shit," she whispered, prompting him to chuckle.

He reached into the nightstand table and withdrew a condom. He'd told her to get on birth control, and suddenly she understood why. She liked the idea of him coming inside her with nothing between them. That might not have been his reasoning. Perhaps he was just ultra-careful about preventing pregnancy.

But she still wanted him without the condom.

Lochlan returned to the bed, resuming his previous place above her, his knees resting on the mattress between her outstretched legs. He kissed her again, a long, lingering, deep kiss that had her temperature rising.

She wrapped her ankles around his waist, trying to draw him closer. He didn't budge; rather, he continued to worship her lips.

Finally, she turned her head to the side, sucking in a deep breath. "Please, Lochlan."

He reached between them, placing the head of his cock at her entrance. Their eyes met, locked, as he slowly pressed inside.

She tried to hide her response, her quiet "oh" that was a combination of wonder and surprise. She was overwhelmed by his size, by how much he stretched her, filled her. It took her a moment to adjust. The man wasn't small anywhere.

Lochlan paused for a second, his brows lowering. She got the sense he wanted to say something, but he didn't. Instead, he moved out incrementally before pushing the rest of the way in.

May expelled a loud breath that was equal parts pain and pleasure.

He kissed her cheeks, his lips touching the shell of her ear as he whispered, "Once we're finished, you're going to tell me something you should have said before."

She frowned, too distracted by how full she felt at that moment to understand. Unfortunately, she didn't have a chance to reply or ask what the heck he was talking about.

Lochlan withdrew until only the head of his cock remained, then he thrust in again, harder, faster. The rough motion hit every single nerve at the same time and her back arched, her body going into overdrive.

"God. Yes," she cried out.

Lochlan lost no time finding a rhythm, both of them greedy, clinging, constantly reaching for more. Her nails scraped the skin on his shoulders as he nipped at her neck, her earlobe.

"Harder," she urged.

He gave her what she wanted and then some, his fingers seeking out her clit, rubbing it until she went over.

May's body trembled so hard from the climax that her teeth rattled. It was painful bliss, agonizing ecstasy.

Lochlan didn't join her. Instead, he pulled out and flipped her to her stomach.

Before she could ask what he was doing, he'd tugged her ass up, her knees on the mattress, holding her lower body up as he slid back inside.

Her inner muscles were too sensitive and she felt another orgasm start to form. Lochlan gave her no reprieve, no quarter, as he slammed into her from behind, the new position driving his cock even deeper.

May white-knuckled the sheets and sank her teeth into the pillow, letting it absorb the sounds of her cries. Thank God the girls were on the other side of the condo.

When she went over again, Lochlan joined her, his body going tight, his motions jerkier, less fluid as he came as well.

Once the storm had passed, May's legs gave out and she fell flat to her stomach. Lochlan rose briefly—she assumed to get rid of the condom—before returning and tugging her back against his chest, spoon-fashion.

"Do you have something you want to tell me?" he prompted.

"That was amazing."

He chuckled. "Try again."

She knew what he wanted to hear, knew what was bothering him, so she turned to face him.

"It's not that big a deal."

"You were a virgin, May."

"Yes, but I'm also not some silly, starry-eyed teenaged girl. I know that sex can just be a physical thing. I don't want you to worry that I'm going to make some big spectacle of this or start declaring my undying love. I'm not."

She thought her response would ease his mind. It appeared to do the opposite. His scowl darkened.

"Fine. Then *I'll* make a big deal of it. I'm glad I was your first. And I'm glad it was amazing."

She smiled as she cupped his cheek in her hand. "It really was."

"Go to Caitlyn's wedding with me."

May shook her head. It was one thing to make this mistake in private. It was another to parade her bad decision out in public. "I don't think that's a good idea."

"Of course it is."

"No."

"Yes."

"You're not going to win this fight, Lochlan."

He gave her a grin that told her he was pretty sure he would. And the second she saw it, she realized he was right.

"Please," she said, uncertain what she was even asking for.

"It's going to be okay, sweetheart. Trust me."

They kissed over and over as the minutes passed. Both of them content to simply look at each other, touch, kiss.

When her eyelids got too heavy to hold open, Lochlan whispered, "Good night."

And she fell sound asleep in a bed that felt like a cloud.

$$\clubsuit \quad 8 \quad \clubsuit$$

ochlan walked into the Grand Ballroom at the Four Seasons with May on his arm, feeling like a million bucks. He was dressed to the nines in a tux and as far as he was concerned, May was, hands down, the most gorgeous woman in the place—after his sister, the bride, of course.

Lucas and Caitlyn's wedding had been beautiful, and now he was looking forward to dancing the night away with May.

She'd taken his breath a few hours earlier when he'd stopped by her apartment to pick her up. For two weeks, she'd offered him every excuse in the book for not attending the wedding as his date, but he'd persisted, efficiently answering every concern.

Linda and the girls were safely ensconced in a room upstairs in the hotel, his response to her final last-ditch attempt—and most likely the real reason she kept turning him down—about not being comfortable leaving the girls alone with her mom so soon after her surgery.

Chloe and Jenny had been delighted when they'd walked

into the balcony room and spotted the harbor. He'd noticed both girls were big fans of the water and made a mental note to follow through on his promise to take them all out on his boat very soon.

Then, in true kid fashion, Chloe had jumped from one bed to the next, giggling and thrilled by the concept of room service.

Lauren had seen Jenny twice so far, and while the young girl still wasn't speaking, May said she felt as though Lauren was making progress. During their last session, Jenny had drawn pictures of her parents and listened as Lauren told her it was okay to feel sad and scared and lonely, that those things were natural and that she had a lot of people around her who would help her through it all. May commented that Lauren was actually helping her, as well, because she'd been guilty of suppressing her own emotions, trying to protect Jenny by not talking about Jeff and his wife around the girls, afraid it would hurt them.

Lately, May had started telling stories about Jeff when they were kids. She had called Lochlan a few nights earlier to tell him that Jenny had smiled at one of her stories. May had been elated, and he had been thrilled she'd wanted to share the moment with him.

"Maybe I should pop upstairs to check on the girls and Mom."

Lochlan wrapped his arm firmly around her waist and continued to propel her toward their table. "Linda would call if she needed you. I'm sure they're fine."

They sat with his parents and Pop Pop during the meal, talking about the wedding and how beautiful Caitlyn looked. Lochlan liked her new husband, Lucas Whiting, quite a lot, something that hadn't been the case when the two of them first started dating.

He told May about Lucas trying to strong-arm the family into selling Pat's Pub by some rather unsavory means.

"That was hardly his worst sin," Pop Pop said.

"He did something worse than that?" May asked, aghast.

Pop Pop shook his head in true disgust. "Lucas is a Dallas Cowboys fan. Can you believe it? A Baltimore boy rooting for Dallas."

May laughed, the response clearly not what she'd expected. "My allegiance rests solely with the Ravens and the Orioles. You have my word on that, Pat."

Pop Pop reached over and patted her hand. "That's because you were raised right."

The music started and because his grandfather was a charmer from way back, he was out of his seat and asking May for a dance before Lochlan could issue his own request.

May blushed sweetly as Pop Pop led her to the floor. Keira excused herself to go talk to her sisters. Lochlan suspected it had killed her to wait through the entire meal before finding her beloved sisters so they could all relive how magical and wonderful the wedding was.

"Looks to me like we won't have too long to wait for another one of these fancy shindigs," his dad said, leaning closer. "You're wearing your heart on your sleeve, son."

Lochlan sighed. "May seems to be the only person who doesn't notice that fact."

"There's a difference between being blind and choosing not to see," Dad said. "From what your mother has told me, May has a lot of responsibilities for someone so young. Caring for her nieces and her mom."

Lochlan nodded. "Plus there's the little issue of me being her boss. She needs the job to support them. She's bound and determined to put the brakes on this, afraid she's risking losing everything."

"And you won't let her."

"I can't, Dad."

"I was your mom's college professor when we met. That was the longest semester of my life, waiting for her to finish the coursework so I could ask her out."

"I'm afraid it's not as easy as waiting a few months for us."

"I know I don't need to issue the warning, but I'm going to anyway. Be careful with her, Lochlan. I don't have a doubt that your intentions are good, that your feelings are sincere. But I've also known you your whole life. May's reasons for being afraid to open her heart are genuine and reasonable. I know you're used to setting a goal and plowing headfirst to achieve it, but this is something you're going to have to let her get to on her own. I tried to force your mom's hand, and I almost lost her because of it."

"Really?" Lochlan had never heard that story.

"You and I are birds of a feather. In a lot of ways. I don't think I have to spell those out for you. I fell hard and fast, and I can see you've done the same. It's going to take May a little longer to catch up because she has more to lose. Remember that, and be patient."

Lochlan sighed. "Patient," he spat out in disgust, prompting his father's chuckle.

"As I recall, you used to utter the words *marriage* and *kids* with that same level of disdain."

"I was a jackass."

Dad didn't disagree. "Yeah, you were."

"Thanks for at least agreeing with the past tense part."

"I'm an English professor, son. If there's something we understand, it's verb tense."

They laughed and lifted their glasses, clinking them together in a toast.

Then the song ended and Pop Pop and May returned to the table. Caitlyn and Mom came over as well.

"It was a great wedding, sis," Lochlan said, standing up to kiss her on the cheek.

"It really was, wasn't it?" Caitlyn's smile lit up the entire room. She looked at May, her eyes widening. "May, you look amazing! I love that dress. Where did you get it?"

May hesitated for a moment, then leaned closer and whispered, "Goodwill."

Lochlan wasn't surprised by her admission. He'd actually thought she would offer the "I have nothing to wear" excuse at some point during her never-ending refusal to attend the wedding. It had never come up. Which made sense now that he thought about it. May's pride was still in full force. She'd never ask for financial help. Ever.

He loved that about her as much as it drove him crazy. He had more money than he would ever need, and he hated seeing the worry lines by her eyes drawn there by an ever-increasing pile of bills. His father's word flashed through his mind.

Patience.

Caitlyn shook her head. "I'm so jealous of people like you. Aunt Riley and Yvonne are just the same. They walk into Goodwill and come out with Kate Spade bags and brand-new jeans with the tags still on them. I go in and can't find anything but faded, stained T-shirts and out-of-style blazers. You'll have to take me with you next time and teach me your tricks."

May laughed. "Deal. Congratulations, Caitlyn. It really was a wonderful ceremony."

"I'm glad you came."

Dad stepped next to Caitlyn. "I want it noted for the

record that I was the first to ask the inevitable question. When are you giving me grandkids?"

"Tacky, Will," Mom murmured as the rest of them laughed.

"It's okay, Mom. Lucas and I have talked about it and we plan to start right away. With any luck, we'll make a honeymoon baby."

Then Caitlyn turned to Lochlan. "So beware, brother dear. Kids are imminent in your life. And I expect you to be a stellar uncle. Endless piggyback rides and epic birthday presents."

Lochlan rolled his eyes, pretending the request bothered him. "So noted."

In truth, all he could think about was his kids growing up alongside his sister's. His cousins meant everything to him, and he wanted his kids to have that same experience.

Caitlyn gave him a sweet wink that told him she knew exactly how he felt and moved on to chat with friends at the next table. A waiter came by with a tray of champagne, and Lochlan grabbed a glass for each of them.

May took a sip, then confessed, "I think I'm already a little tipsy from the two glasses I had at dinner. I don't drink much."

"It's a wedding. You're supposed to drink too much champagne and sleep with the brother of the bride. It's tradition."

May laughed, but someone caught Lochlan's eye by the entrance to the ballroom. "I don't believe it," he murmured.

May turned and followed his gaze. "Who is that?"

Lochlan grinned. "Long-lost cousin."

"What?"

He grasped her hand and crossed the room quickly.

Fergus smiled, aware Lochlan had been the first to see

him. The two of them hugged and, within seconds, the rest of the Collins clan swarmed.

Lochlan stepped aside as Fergus explained his tardiness to the party, something to do with a missed connecting flight and lost paperwork. He was officially out of the Army after two four-year stints, three of those years spent exclusively in the Middle East. The original plan had him home three days ago in plenty of time for the wedding, but Murphy's Law had been in play. Like a true Collins, Fergus was good at making the story an epic tale, filled with adventure, tragedy and humor.

Lochlan rejoined May as they listened.

"Wow," she whispered to him.

"He's the least hard to look at of all of us, but if *you* say that...I might have to kick his ass. Don't make me," he warned.

She made the gesture for locking her lips shut and throwing away the key.

Because it was so adorable, he kissed her.

"Let me guess," she said, the second his lips left hers. He knew what game she was playing. She'd spent most of the day trying to match each of his cousins with their parents. "Fergus is...Sean's son?"

Lochlan shook his head. "Killian's."

She bit her lip, and he knew what her next question would be before she even asked it. "So he's *definitely* Killian's, or...?"

May had been fascinated by Killian's marriage to Justin and Lily. Likewise with Sean's union with Chad and Lauren. He'd worried about her response to their ménage relationships a bit at first. He was very protective of his family, and he would have had a real problem if she'd judged them harshly. Fortunately, she'd been enthralled by the concept, making a joke that Lily and Lauren were probably the luckiest women in the room, teasing him once more about none of the men in his family being hard to look at—Justin and Chad included.

"They've never said who the biological father is, though I'm sure the three of them know. It doesn't matter to any of them—Fergus included. He grew up loving both his dads the same. He looks a lot like Justin, but damn if he doesn't act exactly like Killian."

The rest of the evening passed quickly as Lochlan exposed May to the craziness of a Collins celebration. She'd been in awe when she learned he was related to Sky Mitchell, absolutely amazed and thrilled when she learned Sky and Teagan were going to perform a song at the reception.

"I can't believe this. Do you know how much concert tickets to Sky and Teagan shows are, nowadays? I looked it up once just for shits and giggles. You really *are* related to everyone," she'd teased.

They danced and drank, laughed and talked, and then danced some more. His family had absorbed her into their chaotic, madcap group, and it felt to him as if she'd always been there, or at the very least, as if she'd always belonged there. He always had a great time with his family, but with May, the whole night had been amplified, made a thousand times greater.

"I've never had this much fun in my entire life," she admitted as the evening began to draw to an end. "I'm sorry it's almost over."

Lochlan grasped her hand, tugging her toward him for a kiss. "It's nowhere near over."

He'd intended it to be a quick kiss, but it sparked a flame in both of them.

"Can we go upstairs?" she asked breathlessly.

"I think we'd better. I'd hate to be arrested for public indecency at my sister's wedding."

She giggled as they made a hasty escape. Once they were in the elevator alone together, Lochlan pulled her into his arms and kissed her as if his life depended on it.

They were still locked together when the doors slid open. They parted briefly to make their way to the suite he'd reserved for them. Inside, he pushed her against the wall, tugging down the zipper at the back of her dress as she attempted to push his tuxedo jacket over his shoulders.

They undressed each other with little finesse, working with the shared purpose of total nudity.

"My head is spinning," she confessed. "You. Music. Champagne."

"Maybe you should lie down on the bed," he said with a wink that told her exactly what was going to happen once she got there.

They kissed again as he moved her backwards across the room. Then he pushed her to her back on the mattress, coming over her as her legs parted to welcome him. They hadn't been together since the night he took her virginity. Her mother had been released from the hospital the following day, and no amount of persuasion on his part could convince her to bring her family to stay at his condo. She also wouldn't leave them alone at night since Linda was recuperating. And the two of them definitely wouldn't fit on her couch.

They were quickly coming to a day of reckoning. Lochlan had plans for their future, but convincing May to take the leap wouldn't be easy.

He'd tried to seduce her a couple of times at work, but May held firm to her resolve that they remain professional at the office. Too many times she'd insisted that they would be smarter to return to their roles as boss and employee, but Lochlan refused to accept that.

"Want you," she said, her lips pressed to his. "Want you so bad."

She wrapped her legs around his hips and he let her pull him toward her. He slid inside in one hard thrust. They gasped in unison at the incredible pleasure, then the reins slipped loose. He pounded inside her as she urged him to take her harder. Faster. She came twice in rapid succession. Lochlan managed—just barely—to hang in there, but when her third orgasm struck, he was a goner.

He groaned, his come filling her.

That was when reality hit.

"Did you go to the doctor?"

It took her a few moments to understand his question. "Yes."

He breathed a sigh of relief. "Good. I'm sorry, May. I forgot the condom."

It was apparent she still hadn't realized that, even after his question about her visit to the doctor. "Oh."

Her response triggered a concern. "When did you go?"

"Wednesday."

"Three days ago?"

She nodded. "I got the shot."

"How long before it takes effect?"

"A week."

Lochlan was still inside her. "May—" he started.

"It'll be okay. I'm sure of it. But, um, maybe I should go to the bathroom to wash and jump up and down a few hundred times," she joked.

Lochlan didn't move. He'd spent a lifetime swearing off kids. He waited for panic to creep in. It didn't. Instead, he felt regret for putting May in this situation, and then incredible guilt for hoping he'd just gotten her pregnant.

Jesus. He really *had* fallen fast and hard.

"Are you freaking out?" she whispered.

He grinned. He probably looked like he was. "No, May. I'm not freaking out. Are you?"

"Not yet. But I drank a lot of champagne and just came three times in a row, so I'm probably not in the best frame of mind to think things through."

Lochlan laughed. "God. You're adorable. And perfect."

She rolled her eyes, clearly amused. "I'm so far from both of those things. Lochlan, I'm a mess. We keep making this mistake bigger and bigger."

He hated when she referred to what they shared as a mistake. "It's not a mistake."

"Of course it is. Saying otherwise doesn't change that fact. And it also doesn't make me smart enough or strong enough to stay away from you. I know I should, but...I can't."

"I can't stay away from you either. May..."

It was on the tip of his tongue to tell her loved her. The words were right there, but she spoke first and the moment vanished.

"You never told me why those straps were already on your bed the other night."

He hadn't had the opportunity to talk to her about his dominant tendencies. It was strange. Every sexual relationship he'd had in the past had involved some tenet of BDSM because he desired it. It was what drove him sexually, turned him on.

With May, he didn't need it. He wanted to explore all of that with her, but it wasn't necessary. He was perfectly content to make love to her slow and steady and for hours on end without a single bell or whistle.

"I typically enjoy sex with an edge. Bondage, spankings, rough sex."

"I think I'd like all of that too."

He chuckled. "The first day we met, I noticed something in you, something I tried hard not to see because it spoke to a part of me I keep locked away at work."

"What did you see?"

"Your submissiveness. It called to the dominant inside me."

May frowned, and he wondered if she disagreed with that assessment. Then a sly smile emerged. "And you think you keep that locked away at work? Really?"

He ruffled her hair playfully. "Smart-ass. I'm breaking all the rules with you."

She sobered up, nodding. "Yeah. Me too."

Once again, he felt the overwhelming need to tell her how he felt, but May seemed determined to keep that truth at bay.

"I need to go clean up," she whispered.

He released her reluctantly, watching as she slipped into the bathroom.

Lochlan lay on his back, staring at the ceiling, trying to figure out his next move. His father had waited until Mom was no longer his student before pursuing her, but that wasn't an option for him. Which meant he needed to find another solution. The obvious answer was to convince her to move in with him, to pack up her mom and the girls and live with him in the condo. Hell, at this point, he was ready to buy a proper house for the five of them.

The door to the bathroom slid open and he sat up.

"Hey," she said. "Listen, I've been thinking—"

He didn't like her tone, so he cut her off. "So have I."

"Lochlan—" she started again.

"The ban on office romances is lifted."

She rolled her eyes, laughing lightly. "You're ridiculous."

"Not at all. If you don't want to break a rule, just change it."

"That's not how life works."

He reached for her, pulling her beneath him once more. "It does when you're the boss."

Her lips parted to continue the argument, so he kissed her until the complaint was a distant memory.

"When you come to work on Monday, wear a skirt. And no panties."

"I told you, Lochlan, I'm not having sex with you at the office. It's bad enough I came to the wedding with you tonight. That reporter was there, taking pictures for the social pages. Someone from work is bound to see us in the photos together and—"

"No panties," he repeated. "I'm going to bend you over my desk. I'm going to fill up that tight virgin ass of yours with a butt plug, and then I'm going to fuck you from behind."

May's cheeks flushed as she expelled a quiet, hard breath of air. The image he was painting excited her.

"Please," she whispered.

He wasn't sure what she was pleading for, so he made sure his answer covered it all. "You've taken staying with me at my condo off the table, which means the office is our only option. And I haven't scratched the surface of all the things I'm going to teach you sexually."

"Teach me?"

Lochlan liked drawing pictures for her, liked watching as her eyes went dark with desire, her body tightened with need as he described everything he was going to do to her.

"You're going to suck my dick...tucked away under my desk...*while* I'm in a meeting. I'm going to bend you over every flat surface in that office to fuck you. I'm going to tie you up and make you beg for my dick. Going to put a vibrator inside your pretty pussy, then watch you squirm at your desk when I adjust the speed with the wireless remote. I'm never going to get enough of you, May. *Never*."

"Holy shit." Her curse came out as breath, not sound. "I... God... I need you, Lochlan. Right now."

He didn't need to be told twice. He pressed her legs apart and pushed back inside. This time, they were both aware of the lack of condom. They were throwing caution to the wind, pressing their luck, daring fate.

"May," he murmured as he moved slow and sure, every stroke feeling like pure, agonizing bliss. When it wasn't enough for either of them, he lifted her legs until her knees were tucked over his shoulders. She was bent in half, and the new position allowed him to go even deeper.

She gasped on the first hard thrust, her pussy muscles clenching tight around him.

Lochlan prided himself on staying power, but not tonight. Not right now. Every quiver of her pussy sent him closer to the abyss, until he had no choice but to come or die.

May was with him, calling out his name, her voice hoarse from her cries.

"May," he whispered again as their climaxes began to subside. Her name felt like the answer to a prayer.

He pushed himself to her side, reaching down to pull the covers over their sweat-soaked skin.

She twisted as he wrapped his arm around her waist until her back rested against his chest. They lay together without talking, their breathing growing slower, easier.

He knew the second she dropped off to sleep. He'd been waiting for it.

Because it allowed him to speak what was written on his heart.

"I love you," he whispered.

May rubbed her eyes wearily. It had been a long week after a wild, wonderful weekend. Lochlan had remained true to his word, and each day at work had been a new lesson in kinky fantasies.

The man was seriously fucking with her mind...as well as her body. She left work exhausted yet exhilarated from his daily sexual siege. She should have been able to sleep like the dead each night, but instead, she lay awake, restless, hot and bothered, playing with herself as she lived over each day's wicked adventure.

Now it was Friday, and she was tired and horny. It wasn't a good combination.

Lochlan was out of the office all afternoon for a business meeting, which meant she was also grumpy as hell.

She looked at the clock for the hundredth time in ten minutes. It was just barely past three. The day had already felt like an eternity. She wasn't sure she could survive two more hours.

May stood up and stretched. Time to move or she'd fall

asleep in her chair. She decided to grab a cup of coffee and deliver a stack of files to the CFO. His office was on the opposite side of their floor of the building, and she could use the walk.

She was halfway across the large center space when the sound of someone talking in a hushed voice caught her attention. "...pictures were on that blog I follow. He took her to the wedding."

The speaker was behind a cubicle, unable to see her. Another voice entered the whispered conversation. "Guess that explains how she got the job. Always wondered why he went with someone so inexperienced."

"He's a man," the first person said. "They all think with their dicks."

"Don't be catty, Celia. You're just jealous. You've made no secret of the fact you wouldn't mind spending a little horizontal time with hot Lochlan."

"He's sexy as sin *and* rich. Do you blame me? May moves fast."

May continued walking, her face suddenly on fire. The word was out. Someone had discovered that she had been Lochlan's date for Caitlyn's wedding, and she was office gossip fodder.

Suddenly, she started putting a few things together, things she might have noticed earlier in the week if Lochlan hadn't been distracting her with sex.

Several people had been casting glances her way whenever she walked through the office, giving her knowing grins. One woman had even winked at her, as if they shared some secret. She wasn't sure how she'd failed to put two and two together.

She'd known the pictures of her and Lochlan together had appeared on several Baltimore society sites online. Lochlan had pointed one out to her himself, proclaiming it his favorite picture of them. In it, Lochlan was standing behind her, his arms wrapped around her waist as she glanced back at him, grinning widely.

Her head had been in the clouds, and her body on sex overdrive this week. Constantly. So she'd missed a pretty important fact. The jig was up. Everyone in the office knew about her and the boss.

Chancing a peek around, she noticed no less than three people looking her direction, their eyes lowering quickly when they saw her looking. Or at least that was what it felt like. She was suddenly feeling very paranoid.

She'd neared the CFO's office, but slowed when she heard a couple of men talking inside.

"Can't blame him. She's smoking hot."

She stopped dead in her tracks when Phillip, Lochlan's accountant, sighed. "Maybe so, but I've heard more than a few comments about him breaking the office romance rule."

May took two steps away from the door, then turned and hastened back to her desk. Waves of nausea coursed through her. Any respect she may have earned with the other employees of AdLoch was now gone.

Dropping down in the chair, she sent an email to Lochlan, telling him she wasn't feeling well and that she was going home early. She couldn't stay here, couldn't stand facing down their knowing looks.

When she got home, she'd write up her letter of resignation, give Lochlan two weeks' notice. She'd known when she started fooling around with him that she was risking everything and, like an idiot, she'd done it anyway.

She quickly swiped away a stray tear. She couldn't cry. Not here.

Later, tonight, when she was alone on the couch, she'd

give herself the luxury of sobbing her heart out. Until then, she needed to figure out how to salvage the mess.

First order of business was to find a new job. God, she'd been lucky as hell to find this one. There was no way she'd get another administrative assistant position at this salary, with these benefits. Which meant she was facing a huge pay cut. And a lifetime spent sleeping in the living room.

"What the fuck is wrong with you?" she muttered to herself, falling deeper into a well of self-loathing.

Once she sent the email, she turned off her computer and gathered her things, holding her head high, looking neither left nor right as she walked to the elevator. She wasn't sure if she actually heard someone whisper a comment about her leaving early or if she'd imagined it, but it didn't matter.

May didn't take a breath until the elevator doors closed her in, shut her away from all of them. Then she let a long, shuttering sigh seep out.

"It's fine. It's fine. It's fine," she murmured all the way home.

Her mother was sitting on the couch when she arrived, watching a talk show and waiting for the girls to get home from school.

May tried not to notice that her mother didn't even realize she was home early, just made some sort of rambling comment about one of the guests on the show. May feigned interest, then excused herself to go to the bathroom.

She splashed water on her face and fought down the urge to throw up. Her phone pinged.

You okay?

It was a text from Lochlan. He'd obviously seen her email.

Fine.

She hit send on the text before she realized what she'd done. Time to repair the damage. Fast.

Okay. Not fine. Ate something that didn't agree with me at lunch. No worries.

Lochlan seemed appeased by the quick save.

Need anything? I can stop by after this meeting.

She couldn't see him right now. Her emotions were too close to the surface. If he showed up here, she wasn't sure she'd have the strength to say what needed to be said. She needed the weekend to get her ducks in a row, to gird her loins, so to speak.

On Monday, she would be better prepared to do what she had to do. She'd spend the weekend working on her resume, searching job sites and writing up her resignation. And with any luck, she'd manage to actually get some sleep because she really needed it.

No thanks. Going to drink some ginger ale and turn in early tonight. I'll see you Monday.

Lochlan's reply was longer coming this time. No doubt he didn't like the idea that she didn't plan to see him this weekend. She prayed he'd accept that comment without argument.

I'll call you later.

She rubbed her forehead. She couldn't talk to him.

Really tired. I'll call you tomorrow.

She wouldn't. She wouldn't answer if he called her either.

It was official. In addition to being an idiot, she was a coward.

OK.

May put the phone back on the edge of the sink and did something she never did.

She cried.

LOCHLAN SAT ON THE COUCH IN THE COLLINS DORM AND pretended to watch the football game. He couldn't begin to count the number of Sundays he'd spent in this apartment, surrounded by family, watching the Ravens play. Unlike the majority of his family, he'd followed his father's path, a Steelers fan from the crib, so today's game—between the Ravens and the Packers—held little to interest him. He didn't have a horse in this race.

But he had one in another sort of game. One he definitely felt like he was losing at the moment.

He'd called May earlier to invite her and the girls to join them watching the game, but she said her mother had a migraine and she wasn't comfortable leaving her alone.

He'd known the second she had spoken the words, they were a lie. May was avoiding him, but he couldn't figure out why. The last time he'd seen her had been Friday morning, and it had been his idea of heaven on earth. She'd been sitting on his lap, facing away from him, riding him like a damn stallion. Lochlan had lived the moment over and over no less than twenty times since then.

May was sensual, sexy, an avid student. What she lacked in experience she more than made up for in enthusiasm. And while all of that was wonderful, the woman was also equal parts stubborn.

Which meant she'd dug her heels in on dating him officially. Despite repeated, twelve-times-a-day requests on his part to join him for dinner or on his boat or even just to take a walk on the waterfront, she'd refused. Everyday he'd asked her out, and every single day she'd refused, claiming they'd been lucky no one had discovered she had gone to the wedding with him. It pissed him off every time she mentioned them "dodging a bullet," insisting it was important to her that no one learn of their affair.

He wasn't sure which part of all that angered him more. The fact she thought they'd dodged a bullet, or that she kept calling their relationship an affair.

Fergus dropped down next to him on the couch and handed him a bottle of beer. "That's a hell of a scowl, man. Who pissed in your cornflakes? Ravens are losing. You should probably be the only person here smiling at the moment."

"Yeah." Lochlan glanced at the score on the screen. He hadn't even noticed the Packers had made a touchdown.

"Does your grumpiness have anything to do with that cute blonde you were dancing with at Caitlyn's wedding?"

"May Flowers."

Fergus chuckled. "Not going to lie. That's a pretty awesome name."

Lochlan thought so too, but he couldn't summon the energy to smile. "It suits her."

"Colm and Paddy seem to think you've got it pretty bad for this woman. Never known you to fall in love. Lust, definitely. But not love. You were always too busy trying to make a buck."

He couldn't argue with Fergus. Mainly because what he said was true. Work had been his primary focus since he'd graduated from college and convinced Pop Pop and Dad that he was made to be his own boss. Sometimes he couldn't believe they let him get away with that arrogant bluster, but they had, and he'd spent every second of every day since then with the sole focus of making money, of becoming a success in his field. If anyone had asked him a year ago, he would have sworn he was happy with his life, and he would have meant it with all his heart.

"I don't regret the last ten years, Ferg. In truth, all that work has brought me to a place where I can spend the next forty years or so enjoying what comes next."

"And what's that?"

"Marriage, kids, a family."

"Jesus. I saw some shit in the Middle East that shocked me to the core, but I think what you just said might have overshadowed *all* that."

Lochlan chuckled. "Sometimes I wonder why I come around here so often."

Fergus tapped his bottle to Lochlan's. "Because there's always cold beer."

"You happy to be home?"

Fergus nodded, and Lochlan caught a glimpse of the dark circles under his cousin's eyes. He suspected Fergus's time overseas hadn't been easy. Fergus had trained as a sniper, and up until about a year ago, he'd intended to be a lifer with the military. Lochlan had no idea what had happened to change that, but now wasn't the time to ask. There were too many pissed-off football fans around.

At least until the Ravens scored to tie the game just before halftime and the room erupted in loud cheers. Yvonne stood up and did her touchdown dance, and beer bottles were clinked together.

Typically, Sundays were his favorite day of the week. The one day where he completely put thoughts of work away and enjoyed this time with his family.

Today, however, he wanted to be anywhere else.

No. Not anywhere. He wanted to be with May.

He tugged his phone out of his back pocket. Lochlan didn't like the distance she was putting between them. He was tired of acting like a lovesick fool, letting her call the shots in this relationship. Her continued refusal to date him rubbed against the grain. Time to change direction.

He fired off a text.

Can you come in early tomorrow?

She made him wait a full ten minutes before she replied.

Yes.

He considered warning her that they were going to have a serious talk about their relationship, but he stopped himself. It wouldn't be smart to give her a night to plan her counterarguments.

See you at eight.

It had been on the tip of his finger to remind her to wear a skirt with no panties—the new dress code they'd established this week—but he resisted the urge. He was curious to see what she wore tomorrow, to see how serious she was about building a wall between them.

When she didn't reply, he tucked his phone away and continued to tune out the game, his family, everything.

Instead, he considered what he was going to say to Miss May Flowers.

Because tomorrow, it all changed.

❧ 10 ☙

May beat Lochlan to the office. She had been equal parts relieved and terrified by his request that she come in early. So much so, she hadn't managed to sleep a wink.

She had written up her letter of resignation and arrived at the office an hour before his requested meeting time to print it off. It was currently sitting in the center of his desk—the only piece of paper on the clean surface. May knew she'd never be able to keep her hands from trembling, which meant it was best not to hand it to him. He might misinterpret that as weakness, as a sign she could be convinced to change her mind.

She couldn't.

She sighed, wondering about his request for this meeting.

Had he discovered their affair was public?

She didn't get the sense he cared about that, but maybe he'd changed his mind now that the word was out. He'd made that pronouncement in the hotel room after the wedding about lifting the ban on office romances, but he hadn't put that in a memo and shared it with anyone else.

May sat at her desk, her hands clenched in her lap as she glanced at the clock on the wall again. Quarter to eight.

"God," she murmured. She wasn't sure she could survive another fifteen minutes. She was going out of her mind. She stood and walked to the small kitchenette. Perhaps making the coffee would distract her enough to resist the urge to run away. She hated confrontations.

She'd just finished putting everything together and pushed the on button when she heard a voice behind her.

"You're wearing pants."

May turned around slowly to face him. She'd chosen her outfit with great care this morning.

Lochlan filled the doorway to the room, looking large and intimidating...and sexy as fuck.

She nodded, unable to speak, her mouth suddenly dry.

Lochlan stepped into the small room and shut the door, locking it. "You shouldn't have done that."

She put her hands up, palms toward him, foolishly thinking that would keep the man back. "Wait."

"You avoided me all weekend." His tone was pure accusation.

May shook her head. "No. I was busy."

His eyes narrowed. He recognized the lie. God, he always caught her in them.

Lochlan continued to move toward her until she was trapped against the counter, his body caging her in.

He reached for the first button on her blouse.

She gripped his wrist. "I thought we were going to talk?"

He stilled. "Put your hand down, May."

Lochlan had two very distinct personalities when it came to sex. There was the fun, affectionate lover. And then there was this man. The one who issued wicked demands in a deep dark voice.

She couldn't resist either of them. Obviously. That's why she was in this fucking mess to begin with.

"Lochlan—" she started.

"Put it down *now*," he repeated, his voice louder. Anger had never come into play between them, but there was no denying that in this moment, Lochlan was pissed.

She lowered her hand.

May closed her eyes, struggling to catch a breath. All the air in her body was expelled in quiet, soft pants, but it didn't feel like any was going back into her lungs.

She wasn't sure how much time passed as she stood there, eyes closed, waiting.

Her eyelids flew open when Lochlan cupped her cheek with one large palm. The second she saw his face, she realized the anger had passed. He was back in control. Typical. The man was a master of controlling his emotions.

Meanwhile, she was a whirling dervish, careening madly out of control, constantly.

"We're going to talk about everything, May. But not yet. I can't. You hid from me all weekend."

She didn't bother to deny it. He'd asked to see her Saturday and Sunday, and she'd offered lame excuses to avoid him.

"And you're *still* hiding." His fingers returned to the buttons on her blouse, and she didn't resist this time as he slipped each one free. She'd thought her choice of clothing would make her feel stronger, give her the ability to do what had to be done.

Chalk up another tick mark in the failure column.

Once her blouse was completely open, he slid it over her shoulders but didn't take it off. Instead, he used the material to bind her hands behind her back. Bondage was one of the few things they hadn't experimented with, yet it was the one thing she'd longed for ever since that first night in his bedroom.

Then he reached around her and unhooked her bra. He did some fancy move where he stretched the lacy material over her head, pushing it and the straps down her arms and adding it to the blouse tying her hands.

She wasn't getting loose.

"No more pants," he murmured, his lips moving along her face to the shell of her ear. His breath was hot and she trembled with need.

His comment did nothing to remind her why she was in the pants and to snap her out of this trance. One touch from this man and she lost all common sense.

He unfastened her pants, pushing them and her panties down.

"Step out of them."

She obeyed.

God. She always obeyed.

It was so easy. So hot.

After a lifetime of ignoring her own desires, she didn't have it in her to deny herself this. Him.

Once she was completely naked, Lochlan spun them around, slowly walking her backwards toward the small table in the room. He lifted her up on it, stepping between her outstretched legs.

She wasn't sure she'd ever get used to this feeling of...pure possession. More often than not, their "lessons" involved her being fully naked while he was almost completely dressed.

There was something scandalously sexy about being tied up and draped over this table while Lochlan—hot as hell in his suit and tie—stood over her.

Lord and master.

Her Viking.

The thought prompted a grin.

"Something funny?" he murmured.

She shook her head. This wasn't funny. It was another nail in her coffin. Probably the last.

Regardless, when she was with him like this, she was happy. Beyond all reason and logic.

Lochlan pressed on her shoulders until she dropped back to her elbows, her bound hands resting in the middle of her back. The position thrust her breasts out, which was clearly his intent. He loved them. Told her so all the time. Then proved it by sucking and nipping at them until she was out of her mind.

This time he didn't put his mouth on her. Instead, he reached into his pocket and pulled out a tiny box.

"What is that?"

Lochlan didn't answer. He didn't have to when he opened it and pulled out the first nipple clamp. He'd mentioned them to her before, told her he wanted to use them on her.

She wasn't sure she'd like the sensation, but Lochlan had proven to her several times over that pain could be very pleasurable. May begged for his spankings, the hard heat of his hand—and once a ruler—against her ass driving her to the edge of an orgasm every time.

Lochlan bent forward and roughly sucked one of her nipples into his mouth, the tip tightening, growing. Once he'd awoken the sensitive bit of flesh, he snapped the clamp in place.

She hissed, her lips parting to tell him to take it off.

The brief flash of pain gave way to something better.

He repeated the same things with her other nipple, and

once the second clamp was in place, he straightened up to study his work.

Each clamp had three little beads, and he used those now, tugging on them to increase the pressure, not loosening his grip until he provoked a groan from her.

Her chest rose and fell heavily as her pussy started to clench.

"I need you," she said on a gasp.

"I needed you all weekend. You hid."

Oh shit. Suddenly she realized Lochlan's intent. He would give her pleasure, she didn't question that. But the man was going to make her ache and beg first.

"I'm sorry," she whispered.

He gave her a sweet smile. "I know. But I also know you're a smart woman who thinks that apology will save her. It won't."

She opened her mouth to argue, but it turned into a pained cry when he pulled on the nipple clamp again, reminding her that she was his captive. Her hands were useless to her. She wasn't even sure she could sit upright without his help.

He had her where he wanted her, and he wouldn't free her until his wounded pride was assuaged.

Part of her—the part that pissed her off—actually considered this tiny bit of sensual revenge his right.

She *had* held him at bay. And the hard truth was she intended to make that distance permanent before the end of the day.

So she'd give him his revenge while greedily stealing one more memory for herself.

He continued to play with the clamps, licking and tugging until she was panting, all pride gone.

"Please. I can't take any more."

He wrapped his hand around her upper arm, pulling her to a sitting position on the table. She lifted her legs, trying to use them to pull his hips to hers.

"Inside me," she pleaded.

He chuckled, a dark, humorless, almost dangerous sound, and she knew her punishment wasn't over.

Lochlan lifted her to a standing position before pressing on her shoulder.

"On your knees."

May went without thought. He'd introduced her to blowjobs on Tuesday.

He unzipped his pants, his erect penis level with her face.

She licked her lips. She was a big fan. Especially when...

May leaned forward, intent on taking him into her mouth. That was when Lochlan pulled her hair free of the ponytail and gripped it tightly, using it to guide her, direct her.

She whimpered when he pulled, her scalp burning slightly. She tried to decide if there was anything she liked more than Lochlan's hands in her hair. It was a no-fail turn-on.

He pushed his cock between her parted lips, pushing deep on the first thrust. Lochlan clearly meant what he said about suffering this weekend. He made no attempt to take it easy on her. This was possession—pure and irrefutable.

She loved the guttural grunts and groans she was able to provoke. She nipped at the head of his dick, applying pressure until he pulled her head back.

"Bad girl," he murmured. She smiled and took him back inside, trying but failing to control the pace and rhythm. Lochlan wouldn't give way, his hands in her hair driving the blowjob.

"You're mine," he said, and the words gave her a second's pause. Lochlan must have noticed her hesitation because he pushed in deeper. "Swallow. Take it all."

She was ready.

Lochlan erupted in her mouth, jets of come sliding down her throat.

May moved away as his climax waned, resting her ass on her ankles.

Jesus. What a picture the two of them made.

If anyone walked in at that moment, they'd see exactly what she was trying to walk away from.

May, naked on her knees, bound, as Lochlan, her boss, stood over her, nothing revealed but his cock.

How had she let him take her back here so easily? Without a word of argument or complaint?

She tried to stand. She had to get out of here.

Lochlan reached down and lifted her. Something in her face must've revealed her feelings. She started to step away from him, even as she knew she was helpless to leave. Her hands were tied and her clothing on the floor. Until he released her, she was stuck.

And the man knew it.

"We're not done," he warned her.

She glanced downward, intending to make a face at his soft penis. That failed when she realized the asshole was already growing hard again.

"Seriously?" she said. "Please, Lochlan. You have to under-stand how this looks."

"I know exactly how it looks, but looks are deceiving."

She didn't have a clue how to interpret that.

"This isn't what you think, May. It's not an affair. It's not that goddamn boss-fucking-his-secretary cliché."

It was on the tip of her tongue to ask him what it really was. But she saw that look again. The one she'd dismissed twice before.

Lochlan had feelings for her. Genuine feelings.

She feared the same expression was on her face—they were mirror images in desire and...God help her, love.

But she couldn't give in to that. He didn't want kids. And she already had two.

"Please untie me."

He shook his head. "I can't. You'll run."

She threw her head back, closed her eyes and prayed for the strength to do what needed to be done.

Before divine intervention arrived, Lochlan was there. He twisted her toward the table once more, bent her over it and slammed into her aching pussy from behind. The sound of the clamps tinkled against the table, reminding him they were there.

He reached around her. "Hold your breath."

That was the only warning she got before he removed both clamps at the same time.

"Shit," she breathed, as blood rushed back into the tight tips painfully. Lochlan cupped her breasts with his hands, lightly massaging them until the pain morphed into something better.

Then he started to thrust inside her, pounding deep and hard and true. She came within a dozen strokes. And once that orgasm waned, he pushed her over again in a dozen more.

"Harder!" she demanded, the sound coming out in a snarl. He'd reduced her to a wild beast, only interested in one thing. She needed the pleasure, but God help her if she didn't need the pain too.

Lochlan seemed to recognize that. He released her breasts, using his fingers to pinch her still sore nipples tightly. It was as if he'd pulled the trigger on a gun.

She shoved against him as best she was able, considering she didn't have the use of her hands.

She needed more. "My ass... Fuck my ass." She had no idea where those words came from. While they'd toyed with anal play with his fingers and a small butt plug, they hadn't gone further.

"No."

She tried to shove away from him, intent on forcing the issue. She was completely out of control, but she didn't care.

"No," he repeated, slapping her ass hard. "We don't have lube, and I'm not doing it without. It would hurt."

"I want—"

Before she could finish her thought, her hands were freed as Lochlan loosened the knot in her blouse, pulling it and the bra off. He was still buried deep inside her, but he wasn't moving.

He gripped her wrists, pulling her arms in front of her, both of their upper bodies propped up by their elbows, his chest against her back. She felt the expensive material of his shirt sticking to her sweat-soaked back.

Lochlan pressed a million soft kisses against the side and back of her neck, using gentleness to calm her.

It took several minutes for her head to catch up to her, for her wits to return.

"I don't know...why I acted like that."

She felt his lips tip up in a smile, even as they were still pressed against her neck.

"There's a sex club in town. I'm taking you there."

"That's not funny."

Lochlan pressed his lips against the back of her head. "And I'm not laughing. There's nothing wrong with what you need, what you want. This was my fault. For starting this here. I need you in my condo, May. In my bed. It would take years for me to do everything I want to do with you."

Years.

She started to push up, hoping he'd get the point. He didn't.

"Wait." He withdrew until the head of his cock remained, then he slid back in slowly, every inch reigniting the still sensitive flesh. "One more time."

She didn't bother to pretend she didn't want the same. He took her slowly this time, but the impact was just as powerful. It might have been more potent because he paired his soft lovemaking with the most beautiful words she'd ever heard.

"You're perfect, May. Gorgeous. Smart. You're everything. I can't get enough of you. I never will."

On one last deep thrust, the two of them gave in to the climax. They remained together, leaning over the table for several minutes, long after the sensations had faded.

He was the first to move, rising, then reaching down to help her up. He drew her into his embrace, and once again she was reminded of her nudity, his clothing.

She pulled away, retrieving her clothes. She didn't resist when he helped her dress again, both of them silent, lost in thought.

Once she was put back to rights, May broke the silence.

"Lochlan," she said, unlocking the door, leaving the kitchenette. "We can't keep doing this."

He nodded, shocking her with his seeming agreement. "You're right. We keep risking exposure in a less than ideal way. I'm not happy with carrying on this relationship at work exclus—"

"They know about us," she interrupted, suddenly aware that he didn't know.

"What?" The two of them were walking through her office to his, but Lochlan pulled up short. "What do you mean?"

"I overheard a couple of conversations on Friday. About us."

"I see. And you thought the best way to handle it was to leave work early and hide all weekend rather than tell me?"

It was obvious he didn't think that was right, but she didn't agree. "I wanted some time to figure out my next move."

Lochlan shook his head in annoyance and continued into his office. "*Our* next move."

Lochlan walked behind his desk, obviously intent on issuing some office-wide proclamation, though she didn't have a clue if he was going to lift the ban on office romances, or tell everyone to fuck off about his personal life. His stoic expression revealed nothing.

"I've already fixed it," she said, the moment his eyes landed on the letter of resignation.

He picked it up and read it. Then he balled it up and threw it across the room.

"No. You didn't."

"Yes. I did. This isn't a fight you can win, Lochlan. No matter what you say."

He crossed his arms. "Are you sure about that?"

She nodded, not certain at all.

Especially when he said, "I love you, May."

Too many things crashed in on May all at once. First and foremost was the realization that she loved him too. She'd fallen madly in love with Lochlan.

But that didn't change the rest of the realities smashing into them.

Her mother's dementia. Jenny's silence. Her place here...as his assistant. The fact that she came with two children in tow.

They stared at each other in silence.

He was waiting to hear those same words from her. But was it crueler to say them and drag him into her messy life? Or to remain silent?

Ultimately, the decision was taken away from her. Phillip walked into the outer office and saw her standing in the doorway.

"Hey, May. Is Lochlan in his office?" he asked as he crossed the room to her.

Once he spotted Lochlan, he walked past her. "Good. You're here. I..." Phillip looked over his shoulder at her, before he turned back to Lochlan. "I was wondering if you had a minute. I'd like to talk to you. Alone." He stressed the last word.

May didn't need a college degree to know what this talk was going to be about. She took a step backwards, out of the office.

"May," Lochlan called out.

She shook her head, hoping he could see how much she didn't want him to follow her.

So much for that.

As she continued out of his office, Lochlan was right there, matching her step for step. Once they were out of earshot, she grabbed her purse from her desk.

"Where are you going?" he asked, his voice mercifully lowered.

"Please don't follow me."

"May."

"Please," she repeated, hating the way her voice broke. There were tears in her eyes. She had to get out of here. Fast. "Please."

He pulled up short. "Three days."

"What?" she asked, her eyes on the exit.

"I'm giving you three days to work this out in your head. Then we're going to talk. About *all* of it."

She started to shake her head but his eyes darkened, his jaw clenched. "Three days, May. Not a second longer. Push me on this and I'll start the conversation right now. Right here."

"Three days," she said quickly, simply so she could make good on her escape. Her emotions were off the charts and she needed to leave. Now.

"By the way, you still work here. I'm not accepting that resignation no matter what."

"Three days," she repeated in a whisper, uncertain how to reply to assertion.

He nodded just once, and she could see how much it was costing him to let her go. Her heart broke and her eyes filled with too many tears, her vision blurred.

Before they spilled over, she turned and ran, not stopping until she reached the elevator. Part of her feared he'd follow her.

The other part—the stronger part—feared he wouldn't.

When the doors opened, she rushed inside.

And as they closed behind her, she realized she was alone.

Again.

Lochlan sat in his office, stewing, angry. He'd been in this desk chair, in this frame of mind, for the past three days. Ever since May ran out and begged him not to follow her. Then, like an idiot, he'd given her time to think about what he'd told her.

He should have followed her, pushed the issue, told her he loved her over and over until the words sunk into that stubborn, prideful, beautiful head of hers.

Her crumpled letter of resignation lay on his desk. He'd read the fucking thing a thousand times since Monday, and it *still* pissed him off.

She couldn't leave AdLoch, leave *him*.

He wouldn't let her.

He needed her.

He'd fallen apart in the past seventy-two hours. He'd been late to three important meetings and missed one completely. Two men in the tech department had gotten into a disagreement that had escalated into battle lines drawn, half the office supporting one technician, the rest standing behind the other.

Apparently, the situation had been brewing for weeks, but May had found ways for them to keep the peace. Without her presence, there was a backslide, and he didn't have the energy to even attempt to fix it.

Then he'd spent the better part of yesterday morning looking for a file, only to discover it on top of a stack of folders on May's desk. Right on top. In plain sight.

He ran a weary hand through his hair, muttering, "Fuck."

"Language."

He looked up at the unexpected voice.

"What are you doing here?" Lochlan asked, surprised. Pop Pop didn't drive, and he hadn't been in Lochlan's office in probably close to five years.

"Bubbles is waiting in the car. I asked her to bring me by."

"Why?"

"I was watching you Sunday at the football game."

Lochlan felt guilty. He'd been so wrapped up in his troubles with May, he'd barely said three words to Pop Pop. And he definitely hadn't noticed Pop Pop watching him.

"Why?" He felt like an idiot, repeating the same silly question. He rose and came around his desk, gesturing toward one of the two chairs on the other side.

Pop Pop sat in one, Lochlan the other.

"It occurred to me how much you're like your father."

Lochlan gave him a crooked grin. "That's hardly earth-shattering news. Mom has called me Dad's mini-me since I was five."

"She has, though I never thought the word 'mini' fit in regards to you."

"It's from a movie."

"Ah," Pop Pop said, and it appeared that something he'd never understood suddenly made sense. "I always wondered about that. Well, anyway," Pop Pop reached out and patted his knee, "the Collins family was a bit of a mess when your mom met your dad in his English classroom."

"Our family?" Lochlan found that hard to believe. He'd never met a more solid group of people in his life.

Pop Pop grimaced sadly. "I'm afraid so, my boy. There were a lot of rough years for us after Sunday passed. I had seven kids all under the age of eighteen and a business to run. As a result, a lot of the mothering fell to your mom. She took so much onto her young shoulders. And because I was blinded by grief, I let her. Will was the one who saw how badly she was hurting, but you know your mom. That Collins' stubbornness runs thick in her veins."

"You don't have to tell me. My first name is Patrick. Even though we already had a Padraig."

Pop Pop laughed. "That girl of mine," he said affectionately. "She is a bird in this world."

Lochlan had heard that expression from his grandfather countless times, but he didn't have a clue what it meant.

Before he could ask, Pop Pop continued, "Will fought hard for your mother's heart, but she didn't make it easy on him. She was determined to put her family first, to put our needs above her own. Will taught her that she could take care of herself and still be there for us. I have very few regrets in my life. I've always tried to live in such a way that I could wake up every morning and respect the man looking back at me in the mirror, but I know I failed your mom in those years after Sunday's death."

Lochlan had never heard this story. Had no idea his grandfather had been harboring this guilt. "You wouldn't have changed my mom's need to take care of you all, Pop Pop."

"No. But I should have seen what it was costing her. Will did. And through patience and perseverance, he got through to her. You've got bucket loads of perseverance in you, son."

Lochlan knew where this was going. "It's the patience part that's lacking, right?"

Pop Pop leaned back in the chair. "Half the battle is knowing your own weaknesses. May has a lot of responsibilities for one so young. Like your mother, she's dug in her heels and figured out how to survive. Not live, mind you. Just survive. She needs your patience, your understanding, your love."

Lochlan sighed. "I told her I loved her. She ran away."

"Did you follow her?"

Lochlan realized there was a regret *he* was going to be carrying around for a long time too. He shook his head.

"Take a look at what's holding her back. Start chiseling away at the list. I saw the way that girl looked at you at your sister's wedding. You've already won her heart. You just have to convince her to share the rest—her pain, her stress, her responsibilities, her fears. Love is the easy part, Lochlan. It's the rest that makes life interesting."

"Okay. I'll do that."

Pop Pop pushed up from the chair. "Well, I better get back downstairs. Bubbles was eyeing that fancy bakery across the street from your building. If I leave her alone too long, we'll be toting home three dozen cookies and a mountain of cupcakes." Pop Pop patted his lean stomach. "Can't have that or I'll lose these six-pack abs."

Lochlan laughed. And then he did something he didn't do enough. He reached out and hugged his grandfather. "I love you, Pop Pop."

He was surprised by the strength in the hug Pop Pop returned. "I love you too, son."

Lochlan walked Pop Pop to the elevator, then he took a deep breath.

Time to start chiseling away at the list.

First on the agenda was work.

Lochlan sent out an email, flagging it urgent, and calling an emergency staff meeting. Within thirty minutes, he had ninety percent of the office employees gathered in the conference room. It was a tight fit, but he wanted to make sure the information relayed came from him—and that it wouldn't be misunderstood or misconstrued.

"The ban on office romances is lifted." It was a simple pronouncement and from the grins of at least eighty percent of the faces looking at him, everyone in the joint knew what had prompted his change of heart.

"And I know you all know why. Let me set the record straight on a few things, so the rumors don't include anything that isn't the truth. I didn't hire May. Sally did. I'd never laid eyes on her before her first day on the job here. I'm pretty sure Sally was playing matchmaker."

A couple women sitting near him laughed and one murmured, "That sounds like something Sally would do."

"Her scheme to set me up worked. I'm crazy about May and I'm going to propose to her."

The room—absolutely silent until then—erupted in applause.

He finished up with his hope that she would not only marry him, but continue on as his assistant because he was a mess without her.

That comment got a "hear, hear" from the man who'd had to hold the meeting Lochlan missed on his own. He dismissed everyone back to work, shaking hands with at least a dozen well-wishers. May had clearly misread her colleagues' feelings in regards to their relationship. He would be sure to set her straight on that.

He'd just returned to his office, ready to tackle the next

thing on his list, when his cell phone rang. He picked it up, intent on silencing it, when he saw her name on the screen.

Had someone from the meeting texted her? Told her what he'd said?

"May," he said, thrilled she was calling him. Maybe she'd come to her senses.

"It's Chloe."

Lochlan's stomach lurched even as he grabbed his car keys.

"What is it, Chloe?"

"Can you come over?"

He was already halfway out the door. "Yes. What's wrong?"

"Aunt May is in the bathroom and she won't come out. Nana..." The little girl paused.

"What about Nana?"

"She didn't remember us."

Lochlan was confused. "You mean she forgot to get you off the bus?"

"No. She didn't know who Aunt May was. She kept calling Jenny May and yelling at her for taking a necklace. Jenny started to cry. Then Aunt May started to cry." From the thick sound of Chloe's voice, she was fighting her own tears.

May had been denying Linda's fading grip on reality, unwilling to see the onset of dementia. Not that he blamed her. At twenty-four, May had lost her father and her brother. Admitting her mother's illness would only drive home that she was losing her as well.

"Is your nana okay now?"

"Yes. She went to her room to take a nap and when she woke up, she was back to normal. But Aunt May got sick, and now she's in the bathroom and she won't come out."

There was true terror in the little girl's voice, and it sparked an overpowering determination in Lochlan.

He'd tried to be sensitive to May's fears, but that was over. From this moment on, her family was his. And he took care of what belonged to him.

"I'm on my way, Chloe. You and Jenny hold tight, okay?"

"Okay."

"Do you want to stay on the phone with me?"

There was a pause. "Yes."

Lochlan grinned, delighted that at least one Flowers woman would accept his help. "Okay, that's fine, sweetheart. Why don't you tell me all about your day? How was school?"

The distraction seemed to help Chloe forget to be scared, but it helped him too. He listened to her voice as he drove across the city, anxious to get to May.

Once he arrived, he hung up, parked the car and sprinted up the three flights of stairs.

The state of May's door gave him pause.

The dead bolt was hanging loose, and there was a dent in the middle of the door. A *big* one.

He knocked, and Chloe opened the door, rushing to wrap her arms around his legs. He lifted her up and gave her a hug.

"It's okay, baby. I'm here." He looked around the room, noticing it was in worse disarray than normal. The TV was gone. Actually, it looked like quite a few things were missing since the last time.

Jenny was sitting on the couch, her face pale, her hands balled into fists in her lap.

Lochlan carried Chloe over, the two of them sitting down next to Jenny. "Is May still in the bathroom?"

Chloe nodded.

"And your nana?"

"Reading in bed."

Lochlan sighed. "Okay. Here's what I need you to do. Go to your room and pack bags. Put in as much as you can carry. We'll come back for the rest. You two, your nana and Aunt May are coming to live with me."

Chloe's face lit up and, much to his surprise, Jenny smiled as well.

"For real?" Chloe asked, squirming off his lap, clearly ready to start boxing up the entire apartment.

"Yep. While you do that, I'm going to go talk to your aunt May, okay?"

Jenny and Chloe raced ahead of him down the hallway, disappearing into their room. Lochlan walked slower, trying to figure out how he could convince May to come with him peacefully.

Even though that wasn't exactly necessary. He'd toss the stubborn woman over his shoulder and kidnap her if he had to. She wasn't staying another night in this shithole. For God's sake, not only wasn't there security on the building, now she had no dead bolt on her own front door.

He knocked on the bathroom door. There was no reply, so he tried the knob, surprised to find it unlocked.

May was crouched over the toilet, and it was obvious she had indeed been sick.

He shut the door behind him before kneeling next to her. "May."

She jerked at the sound of his voice, lifting lifeless eyes to his. It had only been three days since he'd seen her, but she appeared to have aged twenty years.

"Lochlan. Go away. I'm sick."

"I can see that. I'm here. Let me help you." He tried to rub her back, but she pulled away.

"No. I'm okay now. It's passed." If she thought that weak reassurance would move him along, she was sadly mistaken.

"What happened to the dead bolt?"

May laughed, but it was a cold, humorless sound. Something Lochlan hated hearing from her. "Someone broke in yesterday while Mom, the girls and I were at the store. I guess if there's a bright side to being poor, it's that there wasn't anything for them to steal."

Lochlan's blood ran cold at the idea of someone breaking in. What would have happened if they'd been home? "That's not funny, May. You could have been hurt."

"It was most likely teenagers," she continued. "All they took were the TVs and some beer from the fridge, a few worthless knick-knacks and my change jar. More the fool them, it was nothing but pennies and nickels."

"Did you call the police?"

She shook her head. Every inch of her body screamed defeat.

His indomitable, powerful woman was broken.

Lochlan felt a bit nauseous himself, seeing her like this.

She moved away from the toilet, dropping to sit on the floor, her back against the bathtub.

Lochlan stood up, rubbed his chin—and then noticed the plastic shopping bag on the counter of the sink.

It was hanging open...wide enough that he could see the unopened pregnancy test inside.

His heart started to race, equal parts fear and hope. While he couldn't think of anything more incredible than May carrying his baby, he suspected she wouldn't view the news as wonderful.

May didn't notice where his gaze had landed. She wasn't looking at him at all. Her eyes were distant as she quietly said, "She forgot who we were." Her voice was weak, tired.

Lochlan knelt down in front of her. "I know. Chloe called."

That admission roused May's interest for a moment, but it was fleeting. She closed her eyes and shook her head.

"I can't do this anymore," she whispered, the words broken. And once spoken, the floodgates opened.

He pulled May into his arms as she sobbed out too many years' worth of sorrow, stress, pain. He held her, rocked her and tried to comfort her with soft words of hope.

"It's going to be okay, May. You're not alone. I'm here. I'll always be here." The tears continued for several minutes and Lochlan simply held her tight, feeling each pained cry like a dagger to his heart.

Finally, when she started to calm, he whispered, "Everything will be fine."

She snorted out a breath of disbelief over his use of her word. "Fine. Yeah. Right."

He cupped her face in his hands. "May. Everything *will* be fine."

"I'm scared."

Lochlan kissed her on the cheek, wishing he knew what to say to make her feel better. Unfortunately, her fears in regards to her mother were genuine. If she was suffering from dementia or Alzheimer's, she was going to get worse, not better.

"I know you are, but you're not alone. You'll never be alone again."

She didn't look convinced. In fact, her face reminded him of her first day in his office. The vulnerability was back.

"I want you to listen to me, sweetheart. And I want you to let the words soak in. You are *not* alone. Everything is going to be all right."

She looked at him and, this time, she seemed to take heart, bolstered by his confidence. "You really think so?"

"I know so."

"How can you be so certain?"

"Because I love you, and I intend to move heaven and earth to make it true."

She bit her lower lip, not responding. But she wasn't running away, like she did the last time he'd told her about his feelings.

Progress.

A solid minute passed, and he lifted one eyebrow impatiently. "You haven't said it back to me yet."

She smiled, and he knew he'd won this skirmish as well.

"Cocky man. What makes you think I'm going to?" she teased.

He crossed his arms. "I'm waiting."

She closed her eyes and sighed, her smile fading. "You don't want me to say it, Lochlan. You really don't."

"Why would you say that?"

"Because I'm a package deal. If I say it back, then you inherit a hell of a lot more than just me in your life."

Lochlan nodded. "I'm aware of that." He stood and pulled her up as well. He wrapped his arms around her in another bear hug, squeezing tight enough that she would know he had the strength to get both of them through this.

"I love you," she whispered.

Lochlan had made millions, seen his company rise through the ranks as one of the most successful tech start-ups out there. All of that paled to the happiness he felt in this moment, hearing those three little words from the woman who'd stolen his heart.

"So here's what happens next," he said. "You, Linda and the girls move in with me."

She started to pull away from him, already shaking her head. He tipped her face up to his with a firm finger under her chin.

"You're moving in, you're marrying me, and you're coming back to work. The condo will work for the five of us until we find a proper house. We're going to find a doctor for your mom, going to make sure she has the best care available."

"You don't want kids," she said, a tinge of stubbornness creeping back into her voice. She may have admitted her feelings, but she wasn't finished fighting completely.

He grinned, her argument weak at best. "I *didn't* want kids. Until you. Now I want to help raise those two sweet girls across the hall and..." Lochlan reached over and pulled the pregnancy test out of the bag. "And I want to make at least three more with you."

"I don't know if I'm pregnant. The nausea could be because of stress."

He'd had the same thought. "Take the test tonight and we'll find out for sure, but understand, I'm marrying you no matter what the results are."

"I'm *not* marrying you." She paused, then a soft grin appeared as she added, "At least not right away. One of has to be practical about this. We've known each other all of two and a half months. Why don't we live together for a little while, make sure we actually like each other before getting hitched?"

"We can discuss that."

She laughed. "How generous of you to allow a discussion. Is this another one of those arguments you don't intend to let me win?"

He gave her a soft kiss on the cheek. "Probably." Then he reached into his pocket and pulled out a small box.

May's eyes widened. "Wait. You came here with a *ring*?"

Lochlan sighed. Clearly May thought his proposal had been issued on a whim. Or worse, as a result of his seeing the pregnancy test. The truth was, he'd bought the ring three days ago, right after she ran out of his office after he told her he loved her.

"Of course I did. When you propose to a woman..." He started to drop down on one knee, but she caught his arm.

"Oh my God. Not here! We're in the *bathroom*. What if our kids ask us one day about your proposal and we have to tell them you dropped to one knee in front of the toilet I was just puking in?"

Lochlan laughed as he stood back up. She'd just given him her answer without realizing it. He could wait for a better place to pop the question and slide the ring on her finger.

"Excellent point. Brush your teeth and meet me in the living room. We're going to pack up as much stuff as we can and get it out of this hellhole tonight."

May hesitated.

"What's wrong?"

"My mom. What if the move confuses her? Makes things worse? Maybe we should—"

"You're not staying here. Period." He reached for his cell phone. "Aunt Lane is a nurse. I'll ask her to meet us at my place after dinner. She can check Linda over, maybe give her something to help her sleep, and then suggest a doctor for us to see in the morning. Okay?"

May nodded, a fresh tear sliding down her face. "That would be really great. Dammit." She tried to quickly swipe it away. "I can't seem to pull myself back together."

He pulled her close and placed a kiss on top of her head. "So you'll hang on to me until you can."

For the first time, May did just that. Let him guide her and her family through what came next without complaint. Within two hours, Lochlan had her, her mom and the girls packed up and moved into his place. They'd ordered pizza, eating it in the living room, despite May's concerns for

Lochlan's furniture. He insisted leather was easy to clean, and they had a picnic around the coffee table and his big screen TV, calling out letters and guesses to *Wheel of Fortune*.

Lane arrived and spent nearly an hour chatting with Linda. When she left, she gave them the number of a doctor who specialized in treating dementia patients. Her mother retired after the visit, marveling over the comfortable bed in the guest room and thanking Lochlan for the hundredth time for offering them a safe place to stay.

May's fears regarding the move confusing her mother never materialized. If anything, she seemed more at ease, more relaxed than Lochlan had ever seen her.

They walked toward the girls' room hand in hand.

"She never mentioned feeling unsafe in our apartment," May remarked.

"I suspect she didn't want to upset you. She knew you were doing everything you could to keep all of you in a home and fed."

She stopped him just outside the girls' room. "Lochlan, I overheard those people at work talking about us. I don't know how to convince them that I'm not just after your money with all of us moving in here like—"

Lochlan placed his index finger over her lips. "Stop. Don't even finish that thought. None of them feel that way. Besides I've set the record straight and they're happy for us. Genuinely happy."

"Oh."

"You can't resign, May. I'm completely inept when it comes to dealing with anything in that place."

She laughed. "I doubt that."

"If you feel better, I'm dragging you back to work tomorrow. You'll see for yourself. I'm not a pretty sight when left to my own devices."

"Okay."

"Really?" he asked.

"You've given me a safe place to live. The least I can do is kick your ass into shape at work."

"There's my feisty girl. I was starting to wonder when she'd reappear."

He kissed her, intending to make it a quick, short buss, but the second his lips touched hers, things got out of control. One minute, he was giving her a friendly kiss, and the next, he had her backed up against the wall, his hands creeping under her shirt.

"We better put the girls to bed," he murmured against her lips. "And move this to the bedroom. Quickly."

May was out of breath when they parted, so she took a moment to compose herself and then they walked into the bedroom.

Chloe was bouncing on the bed, still full of way too much energy this close to bedtime. "Is this *really* going to be our room?"

Lochlan nodded. "Yep. All yours. We can redecorate it however you want. Replace that big bed with twin beds or bunks even, if you'd like."

"I like the big bed and sleeping with Jenny."

Lochlan knew that wouldn't always be the case, but considering the life-altering changes they'd gone through in the past year, he understood the sisters' desire to hold on to each other—the only constant.

"Well, then," he suggested, "how about a new paint color and bedspread?"

"Pink!" Chloe shouted.

Lochlan started to agree when another voice piped up.

"Purple," Jenny corrected quietly.

May looked at Jenny, then him, then back at the young girl again in complete disbelief.

As always, it was Chloe who never missed a beat.

"Yeah! Purple!" She grabbed Jenny's hands, and the two of them giggled as they jumped on the bed.

It took May a full minute to comprehend what she was seeing—and then she was on the bed as well, laughing and tickling both little girls.

Lochlan watched, his future unfolding before his eyes.

It had never looked better.

$$\text{\textbf{\textit{12}}}$$

Lochlan carried May over the threshold to his condo as she laughed. The girls were having a sleepover at the Collins Dorm with Yvonne, and Lochlan's mother had invited Linda to stay at her house so the lovebirds could spend their wedding night alone together. Keira was aware of Linda's fading memory and had promised to keep a very close eye on her.

Only three months had passed since Lochlan had swept into the bathroom at her apartment and whisked her here. After putting the girls to bed that first night, Lochlan had led her to the living room, where he'd dropped to his knee to propose in a much more romantic setting.

She'd said yes. And then he waited while she took the pregnancy test.

As Lochlan put her down, she rubbed her hands over the small bump forming as the baby grew inside her.

It amazed her to think how, in one night, she'd gone from feeling as though she'd lost everything, to suddenly getting every single thing her heart desired. A home, a husband, medical care for her mother, Jenny's voice back, her job, and a baby. Talk about a sliding-door moment. It had been magical, perfect. And it had only gotten better each day since.

Lochlan had wanted to plan a big wedding, an event to rival Caitlyn's, but May put her foot down, insisting on something smaller, more intimate. She was delighted to have finally won an argument.

So today they'd headed to the Justice of the Peace with her mom and the girls, Lochlan's parents, his sister and Lucas, and his Pop Pop. The simple ceremony had been sweet. Perfect. Now that she'd opened the floodgates, the tears she'd struggled to shed for years appeared regularly these days... provoked not by sadness, but by genuine, overpowering happiness.

After the ceremony, and because the Collins family never passed up an opportunity to celebrate, they left the courthouse and traveled to the pub. Lochlan's aunts and cousins threw one hell of a wedding reception.

Best of all, Sally had surprised both of them by showing up. When Lochlan cornered her to ask if she'd been playing matchmaker, she admitted she had hoped something might spark between them, but she hastened to add if it hadn't, he still would have gotten a great PA. Lochlan had kissed his old assistant on the cheek, then bought her a beer.

"Start taking off your clothes, Mrs. Wallace. I want you naked by the time we reach the bedroom."

May stopped. "May Wallace," she said, crinkling her nose. "Kind of boring and normal."

Lochlan laughed. "You want to keep your maiden name? Or hyphenate? I don't mind either way."

She reached up, wrapping her arms around his neck to kiss him. "I'm only kidding. I love the sound of May Wallace."

"So do I. But...you're not walking to the bedroom. Or undressing."

"Has anyone ever told you that you're impatient?" she teased, even as she started unbuttoning her silk blouse.

"Only everyone I've ever known." Lochlan's eyes drifted lower, watching as she gave him a sexy striptease, slipping each button free slowly, tempting him with only glimpses of her lacy pushup bra.

Once her blouse was open, she turned her back to him, sliding the silk over one shoulder, then the other.

She let the slick material fall to the ground, but she made no move to face him. Instead, she reached behind her back, unfastening her bra. Holding the cups in place, she spun around and let it drop as well.

Lochlan's eyes never left her body, taking in every inch of what she revealed.

May reached for the zipper on her skirt, taking her time as she dragged it down. A quick glance below Lochlan's waist told her he was enjoying her show...a lot. His pants were bulging and he made no attempt to hide the raging hard-on inside.

She shouldn't have looked down. Suddenly, teasing him with a slow show felt impossible. She shimmied her skirt and panties to the floor, kicking both off, along with her heels.

Lochlan chuckled as he approached her. "Looks like you're suffering from a case of impatience yourself."

She expected him to kiss her, so she was surprised when he knelt in front of her instead, placing his lips on her stomach, kissing the tiny bump. May ran her hands through his hair.

When they'd read the results of the pregnancy test and seen the plus sign, May's first reaction had been outright panic...even with the engagement ring on her finger. Everything had gone so fast between them, and every now and then she still had brief moments of fear. She'd lived under a dark cloud for most of her adult life, so she struggled to believe good things could last.

She'd shared that fear with Lochlan, who'd promised to spend the rest of his life proving her wrong about that.

She hoped he succeeded.

"I can't wait to meet you," Lochlan whispered to the baby inside her.

May grinned. "You realize there's a fifty/fifty chance there's a girl in there. Think of how outnumbered you'll be then."

Lochlan had joked the other day about feeling as if he'd suddenly moved into the Barbie mansion, his masculine abode suddenly dripping in "girl stuff."

Of course, May had pointed out that *he'd* created that environment, spoiling Chloe and Jenny, constantly stopping to buy treats and toys for them—dolls, LipSmackers, even little parasols—just because.

"I'd love another girl, May."

She ran the back of her hand along his beloved face as he looked up at her.

"I think I'd like a little boy," she admitted. "This world needs more men like you. Knights."

"Vikings," he corrected.

"Protectors and conquerors."

He'd warned her that he wanted to conquer her, and she couldn't deny it felt as if that was exactly what he'd done. Funny how the words sounded like something negative, when in truth it was the most beautiful thing she'd ever experienced. "You've given me so much, Lochlan."

He stood up. "If you're doing that damn tally in your head again, trying to decide if it's equal, you can stop right now. I'll never be able to give you back a tenth of what you've given me...what you're giving me right now." As he spoke, he rubbed his hand over her belly.

May curled into his arms, loving the way it felt to be completely wrapped up in Lochlan's warmth. "I suck at understanding unconditional love, don't I?"

He kissed the top of her head. "You'll get there. I'm not worried about that."

She lifted her face, wanting him. One look in his eyes told her he wanted the same.

May leaned forward, rising on tiptoe for a kiss, but he shook his head.

"Bedroom," he whispered as he grasped her hand and tugged her down the hallway, not stopping until they were next to the bed.

She sat on the edge of the mattress, holding her hand out to him.

"I think maybe I'd better lose some clothes too."

Lochlan treated her to her own striptease, tugging his tie free from his collar. He reached for her wrists, loosely binding them together in front of her. She could slide the silk off easily, but she didn't make the attempt. She knew this bondage was more for aesthetics than capture, especially when his eyes darkened with hunger.

He shed his shirt, then slid his belt out of the loops. Lochlan bent the leather in half, slapping it against his leg.

She giggled. He loved to tease her with the threat of his belt, especially when she was being a brat in bed, but he'd never followed through on it. He rolled his eyes at the sound of her laughter before tossing the belt to the floor.

"One day," he murmured.

"Promises, promises," she whispered in return.

Lochlan took off his pants, boxers and shoes without

fanfare, pressing her legs apart as he knelt between them. Gripping her ass and tugging her to the edge of the mattress, his mouth was on her clit in an instant.

May gasped, her head thrown back as sparks flared, her body humming with pleasure. It hadn't taken Lochlan long to find all her hot buttons. He sucked her clit roughly, and then nipped at the distended flesh as she cried out, begging for more.

He dipped his tongue inside her, fucking her with it as she gripped his hair, pulling it in a desperate attempt to keep his mouth on her. Not that he was going anywhere. Lochlan was a master of foreplay. Actually, he was a little *too* good. Too many nights he'd keep her on the edge of an orgasm for hours, until she was covered in sweat, struggling to breathe and begging hoarsely for completion.

"Lochlan," she said after several minutes. She needed more, and he knew it.

"Yes, Mrs. Wallace," he murmured, the vibration of his voice adding another sensation to the mix.

She shivered, loving the sound of her new name.

"Come inside me."

Lochlan stood and watched as she scooted to the middle of the bed, then he followed her, caging her beneath him.

"I love you," he whispered as he placed the head of his cock at her opening.

"I love you too." She tried to recall why it had been so difficult to say those words the first time. Now they flowed out of her like the most natural thing on earth.

He pressed in slowly at first, but neither of them was ever satisfied with that for long. Their lovemaking grew wilder with each encounter, both of them turning into ravishing beasts. May joked that every time with him felt like an out-of-body experience. She'd thought that would make him laugh, but he'd only agreed, claiming that was the best description of it for him as well.

She came twice, both times the pleasure roaring through her like a freight train, loud, powerful, earth-shaking.

Lochlan slowed his thrusts, kissing her deeply, gently.

"Lochlan," she whispered.

"Shhh. Let me love you, May."

He punctuated his request by pressing in as far as he could go, then holding still. She loved being filled with him, loved having his baby inside her, loved being his wife.

Lochlan had given her things she'd never let herself dream of.

He pulled out leisurely, the deliberateness of his actions driving her as wild as his rough, hard thrusts.

He continued to move in and out as if they had all the time in the world. And it occurred to her that they did. A lifetime in fact.

Lochlan stroked her clit when he got close to the pinnacle, determined to take her with him. He didn't need to worry. She was there too.

She gasped as she came again, Lochlan jerking roughly above her with his own climax.

He kissed her once more before lying next to her, his hand resting on her stomach, his thumb idly stroking up and down.

May gasped, pressing both her hands over his. "Did you feel that?"

"No, what is it? Are you okay?"

"I think...I think I felt the baby."

Lochlan put his chin on the mattress and peered at her stomach.

She laughed. "I don't think there's anything to see yet. But there will be."

"And I can't wait."

EPILOGUE

Lochlan sat in one of the chairs in Pop Pop's room at Riley's house and sighed. Little Wyatt was in his great-grandfather's arms, sound asleep. The two of them were chatting in this quieter corner of the house, as May and the girls were in the kitchen with Riley and Bubbles, baking cupcakes for the Fourth of July picnic they were all attending on his boat tomorrow.

Pop Pop ran the back of his finger along Wyatt's cheek and the infant grinned in his sleep.

"My first great-grandchild."

Lochlan heard the wonder in Pop Pop's voice, connected with it, felt it.

"I've done nothing but look at him since he was born. I can't quite believe..."

His grandfather gave him an understanding smile. "That he's yours. That you brought this beautiful, wonderful creature into the world."

Lochlan nodded. "Why did I think I didn't want this?"

Pop Pop laughed. "I never believed you'd hold firm to that

no-kids comment. You've always had too much to give to keep it all locked up inside. Look at the difference you've made in those young girls' lives. Jenny was silent when you first brought her around. Now it's hard to get a word in edgewise around her."

Lochlan chuckled. Truer words were never spoken. It was as if Jenny had spent every minute since saying the word "purple," making up for lost time. Not that the transition had come quickly or easily. When they'd called Lauren to tell her about Jenny's one spoken word, she'd insisted on seeing her. Jenny had actually gone silent again for about a week, but on the next visit to Lauren, the words came back...along with the tears and fears and pain.

Since then, Lauren had begun to talk with Jenny and Chloe individually, then the two girls joined May in a family session where they shared their grief and fears.

"She's amazing," Lochlan said, recalling Jenny describing the special red, white and blue cupcakes she planned to decorate today with Aunt Riley's help. Her enthusiasm had been so contagious, Lochlan had been tempted to join them in the kitchen himself.

"I wonder if you might do something for me, son."

Lochlan nodded instantly. There was nothing his grandfather could request that he wouldn't deliver on. "Of course."

"There's a frame over there I need help putting back up on the wall."

Lochlan glanced over at his Pop Pop's "family" wall, the entire thing covered with photographs of every single one of his children and grandchildren. He noticed the photo of himself—grinning like a fool while holding up the *Forbes Magazine* with AdLoch featured on the cover—was gone. It had hung there for well over five years.

"I got a new picture?"

Pop Pop didn't reply, just nodded his head toward the table.

Lochlan rose, smiling when he saw the recent picture. It was an impromptu family portrait, snapped by his mother the day they came home from the hospital with their son. Chloe was holding Wyatt, very carefully, as Jenny and May flanked her on the couch. Lochlan was perched on the arm of the sofa, and all of them were looking at the new baby.

"I like that picture," Pop Pop admitted. "Like replacing my workaholic grandson's photo with one of his new family."

"Instant family," Lochlan joked as he put the frame back in its rightful place. He took a moment to admire it, recalling how his heart had been so full that day, he'd thought it might burst.

Then he studied the other pictures, noticing that quite a few of the frames held newer pictures. Caitlyn's now contained a photo of her and Lucas dancing at her wedding. There was one of Hunter, singing onstage as Ailis stood just at the edge of the curtains backstage, watching. The spotlight was on Hunter, but the camera's focus was on Ailis. He swallowed down the lump in his throat when he saw Padraig and Mia's picture, the two of them looking at each other, ignoring the rest of the world. He missed the kind woman.

His eyes traveled over the wall, and he realized that in every single one, Pop Pop had captured the same thing.

Love. In all its many forms.

He started to remark on it, but Pop Pop spoke first, talking not to Lochlan, but to the sleeping baby in his arms.

"*Och*, wee Wyatt. What a strong name for a strapping lad. Your parents named you well, my little warrior. I can just imagine your future..."

Lochlan stood quietly, listening as Pop Pop whispered to Wyatt about the importance of his name and family.

And love.

I hope you enjoyed this first book in the WILDER Irish series. Why not dive all the way in? The next book, Wild Kisses, is available now.

Have you read the entire WILDER IRISH SERIES? ALL the books are standalone, so they can be read in any order. Be sure to check out all of them!

Wild Passion
Wild Desire
Wild Devotion
Wild at Heart
Wild Temptation
Wild Kisses
Wild Fire
Wild Spirit
Wild Side
Wild Night
Wild Embrace
Wild Dreams
Wild Chance

FANS OF WILD IRISH AND FACEBOOK! THERE'S A GROUP for you. Come join the Wild Irish Facebook group for sneak peaks, cover reveals, contests and more! Join now.

BE SURE TO JOIN MY NEWSLETTER FOR A FREE WILDER Irish short story, One Wild Night.

· · ·

Turn the page to read an excerpt of WILD KISSES, available now.

WILD KISSES

"Landon, listen—"

She was going to argue about it. Of course she was. It was what Sunnie did. For a young woman, she was a dangerous blend of opinionated and confident. It meant winning fights with her took tenacity.

"You don't know a thing about me when it comes to my tastes in women," he assured her.

She started to speak, but he cut her off again when he added, "Or what I like in bed."

That caught her attention. Her eyes narrowed briefly, in shock, then she tilted her head, and he knew he'd piqued her interest.

"Like what?"

He grinned, and the words—freed by tequila and beer and too many nights alone with his hand—came easily.

"I like being in charge in the bedroom, directing everything that happens."

"Like what?" she repeated, stressing the words, wanting more details. She was clearly fascinated.

"I like playing with a woman's breasts, sucking on her nipples until they're hard, bending her over my lap and spanking her ass, tying her up and going down on her, throwing her legs over my shoulders and fucking her like there's no tomorrow...and then flipping her to her stomach and taking her ass the same way."

Sunnie's mouth fell open, and Landon tried to figure out if it was absolute shock or utter horror driving the response.

"Holy shit," she whispered, then she leaned closer, scrutinizing his face. "You're drunk."

He nodded. "So are you."

Their faces were mere inches apart—and that was when it hit Landon.

Hit him like a ton of bricks.

He wanted to kiss her.

He wanted to kiss Sunnie Young.

He'd never in a million years felt that desire, never even considered it.

She was Finn's kid sister, a pain in the ass. To quote her *and* Snoop, too wild, too young, too free. She was the opposite of what he looked for in a woman.

Maybe that explained a lot about his single state.

Jesus. He really *was* drunk.

Time to retreat and revisit this tomorrow without the tequila flowing through his veins.

And he would have done that.

If Sunnie hadn't licked her lips and moved closer.

"Is that really what you like?" she whispered.

He nodded, then Landon met her halfway, his lips touching hers, their tastes identical—the perfect blend of bacon and tequila.

Sunnie kissed like she did everything else in life, with exuberant enthusiasm. Her tongue was in his mouth, her arms wrapping around his neck. He reached for her, his fingers touching her bare midriff, the temptation to move higher to her breasts taunting him.

He was vaguely aware of his surroundings and—

"Sunnie? Landon? What the fuck, man?"

Landon jerked back at the sound of Finn's voice. It took him a second to clear his vision. Sunnie seemed to be struggling to do the same.

Then she moved back, looking adorably confused and... dammit...regretful. *Oops*, she mouthed.

Wild Kisses is available now!

ABOUT THE AUTHOR

Virginia native Mari Carr is a New York Times and USA TODAY bestseller of contemporary romance novels. With over two million copies of her books sold, Mari was the winner of the Romance Writers of America's Passionate Plume award for her novella, Erotic Research. She has over a hundred published works, including her popular Wild Irish and Compass books, along with the Trinity Masters/Masters Admiralty series she writes with Lila Dubois.

Find Mari Carr on the web at
www.maricarr.com
mari@maricarr.com